Slowly, Natty Unfolded the Letter . . .

"Dear Natty," it said. "I got a job at a lumber camp in Washington State. They're shipping me out today. I wanted to see you first, but maybe that would've been tougher. I'll send for you as soon as I can. Love, Dad."

At first, Natty couldn't believe it. He was really gone. Then she knew what she had to do. She couldn't just stay in Chicago and wait. She had to go to Washington and find her father. They belonged together. And nothing—not thousands of miles of country with no easy way to cross it—would keep Natty Gann from being with her father again.

WALT DISNEY PICTURES PRESENTS

The
JOURNEY
of
Natty Gann

A LOBELL/BERGMAN PRODUCTION
A JEREMY KAGAN FILM
Produced in Association with
SILVER SCREEN PARTNERS II
Starring MEREDITH SALENGER,
JOHN CUSACK, RAY WISE
Production Designer PAUL SYLBERT
Director of Photography DICK BUSH, B.S.C.
Written by JEANNE ROSENBERG
Produced by MICHAEL LOBELL
Directed by JEREMY KAGAN
Distributed by BUENA VISTA
DISTRIBUTION CO., INC.
© 1985 Walt Disney Productions

Most Archway Paperbacks are available at special quantity discounts for bulk purchases for sales promotions, premiums or fund raising. Special books or book excerpts can also be created to fit specific needs.

For details write the office of the Vice President of Special Markets, Pocket Books, 1230 Avenue of the Americas, New York, New York 10020.

The
JOURNEY
of
Natty Gann

A NOVEL BY ANN MATTHEWS

**Based on the motion picture from
Walt Disney Pictures**

Produced by Michael Lobell
Written by Jeanne Rosenberg
Directed by Jeremy Kagan

AN ARCHWAY PAPERBACK
Published by POCKET BOOKS • NEW YORK

This novel is a work of fiction. Names, characters, places, and incidents are either the product of the author's imagination or are used fictitiously. Any resemblance to actual events or locales or persons, living or dead, is entirely coincidental.

AN ARCHWAY PAPERBACK *ORIGINAL*

An Archway Paperback published by
POCKET BOOKS, a division of Simon & Schuster, Inc.
1230 Avenue of the Americas, New York, N.Y. 10020

ISBN: 0-671-60649-2

First Archway Paperback Printing October, 1985

10 9 8 7 6 5 4 3 2 1

AN ARCHWAY PAPERBACK and colophon are
registered trademarks of Simon & Schuster, Inc.

Printed in U.S.A.

IL 5+

Introduction

It was Chicago. The year was 1935, and the United States was deep in the Great Depression. Thousands of people were out of work. Parents couldn't support their children. Orphans ran through the streets of the city. Every day, whole families were turned out of their homes when they could no longer pay the rent. With no place to go, they sat in the streets surrounded by their belongings, their faces hopeless and tired.

In those hard times, people—children as well as adults—often gave up and took off in search of something better. The country was swarming with hobos and orphans and runaways. They traveled across the land, working for their meals, walking mile after mile, or hopping on trains and hiding in boxcars for a free ride.

1

Their lives were sometimes exciting but often dangerous.

Natty Gann was thirteen years old in the summer of 1935. She and her father, Sol, were a little better off than some people. At least they still had a place to live—the dingy San Marco Hotel. Sol had lost his steady job, but he still found occasional work, just enough to support himself and Natty. Most importantly, Sol and Natty had each other. And that was really all they wanted. . . .

Chapter One

The meeting hall was crowded. More than two hundred out-of-work men had stuffed themselves into the hot, smoky room. They talked and argued and shouted. They wanted their jobs back, but they knew there was little hope. Times were too hard. The bosses couldn't afford to pay the workers. But the workers had families to support.

In the front of the room, the moderator was losing his patience. The meeting was getting out of hand. Nothing was being decided. "All right! All right!" he yelled, trying to make himself heard above the din. "Shut up for a second, will ya? Sit down, all of ya."

Nobody paid any attention to him. The moderator scanned the room, hoping for some kind of help. It came when a rickety wooden elevator sank slowly to the floor at the back of the meeting room, and the doors slid open. When the moderator saw who had arrived, his eyes lit up. "Hey, Sol!" he cried. "Sol! Get up here."

A murmur ran through the crowd. The men turned to see Sol Gann, a solid, rugged man, who somehow managed to stay calm in all the confusion. Sol was important to the workers. He knew what their rights were, he knew when things were unfair, and he stood up for what he believed in. He was serious and honest, and the men looked up to him.

Behind Sol was his daughter, Natty. Beaming with pride, she shoved him toward the podium, watching as the crowd made way for him. "Go get 'em, Dad," she told him.

Natty thought her father was just about the handsomest man in the world, and certainly the best dad. She thought he was better looking than any movie star, and she even dressed like he did. That evening, she was wearing worn trousers, a leather jacket, and an old cap with a big visor. The sparkling blue eyes that looked out from under her short, unkempt dark hair, were wiser than her thirteen years—and pretty, too, but she wouldn't have believed that. Natty's life with Sol was loving, but her Chicago world was tough, and Natty had a lot more than her appearance on her mind.

For a while she paid attention to the meeting.

Sol took his place at the podium in the front of the room. He searched the faces of the men in the crowd. He wanted to reassure them, but he didn't have good news. He'd just come from a meeting with the bosses, and it hadn't gone well.

"We talked to them," Sol said. "But they won't give an inch. Fact is, they're going to lay off more guys."

"They can't do that!" the men shouted angrily. "We ought to hang them! Burn the place down."

"That won't feed your kids," said Sol quietly. The men were in trouble, and Sol knew it. He also knew that violence wouldn't give them their jobs back.

"So what are we supposed to do, Gann?" someone shouted from the crowd.

"Talk to them," replied Sol. "Let them know we're working men and proud of it. We want to work. We need to work. We deserve to work."

The crowd quieted down. Some of the men murmured their agreement.

The meeting went on. Natty grew bored. She'd heard it all before. She signaled to a friend of hers, sitting next to his father in the crowd. "Psst. Hey, Louie. Psst."

A boy Natty's age turned around. Natty signaled to another friend, Frankie, and the

5

boys left their places and followed Natty into the men's room.

The three of them crowded into a stall and slid the latch shut.

"Got it?" Frankie asked Natty.

"Sure I got it."

"Let's see."

Natty reached into her pocket and brought out a cigarette.

"Hey, she got it." Louie sounded impressed.

"I said I would." Why was it, Natty wondered, that boys never thought girls could do anything daring? She turned to Frankie. "You got the matches?"

Frankie looked sheepish. He patted one pocket after another, checking carefully, even though he knew he didn't have any. He shrugged his shoulders. "I forgot."

Natty shot him a look of disgust. "Figures," she said. She reached back into her own pocket and triumphantly pulled out a match. Then she lit the cigarette and handed it to Frankie.

Suddenly, the door to the bathroom opened. Natty heard footsteps approach. She and Frankie and Louie immediately grew silent. They waited. When the man finally opened the door to leave, Natty could hear her father talking in the meeting room.

"If you're working hard," Sol was saying,

"you ought to be paid for it. An honest wage for honest work."

The door closed.

Louie looked at Natty. "Your dad's really giving it to 'em. He always knows what to say. He makes them see all sides of things."

"Yeah."

Frankie looked skeptical. "My dad says your dad's a Red," he said. "Says they ought to ship him to Russia 'cause he's a Commie."

"Huh?"

"Says they ought to ship him to Russia 'cause he's a Commie," Frankie repeated, taunting Natty.

"He is not!" she cried.

"My dad says he is."

"Well, your dad's as dumb as you are."

"You calling my dad dumb?" asked Frankie.

"You calling my dad a Commie?"

"Yeah! You want to make something of it?"

Natty didn't bother to answer. She drew her fist back and slugged Frankie in the stomach. He staggered, then leaped at Natty. They rolled out of the stall and across the bathroom floor, hitting each other, as Louie tried to break them up.

"Hey! Knock it off," he shouted. "Frankie! Natty!"

The noise brought several of the men from

the meeting room. With some difficulty, they managed to pull Frankie and Natty apart.

Later that night, Natty sat on the lower edge of a bunk bed in the room she and Sol lived in at the San Marco Hotel. It was a sad old room, crowded and cluttered with knickknacks. The paint on the ceiling was cracked and chipped. The wallpaper was faded and stained yellow in spots, but Natty had covered most of it with photos of baseball players and boxing champs. A broken chair leaned into a corner, and the dresser was battered and missing its knobs.

Sol sat in front of Natty, delicately dabbing at her bruised face with a dampened towel. Natty grimaced, but she refused to cry. Besides, she was secretly proud of her fight.

"Want to talk about it?" Sol asked gently.

Natty shrugged and stared at the floor.

Sol nodded, resigned. Then he leaned back to get a good look at her face. "I think you'll live," he said.

Natty attempted a smile. Then she asked, "Dad? What's a Commie?"

"Is *that* what you were fighting about?" Sol had known he'd find out sooner or later, but Natty's question surprised him.

"Frankie says you'll go to Russia because you're a Commie," Natty said. "Are you?"

"Going to Russia?" Sol joked.

But Natty was in no mood for jokes. She couldn't believe her father would do anything wrong, and she desperately needed to hear his answer. "You know what I mean," Natty replied. "Are you?"

Sol laughed. "No. I'm no Red. I'm just standing up for what I believe."

"Me too," said Natty.

"In the men's room?"

"It's as good a place as any."

"Maybe you should stop wearing pants."

"Come on, Dad."

"I don't know if your mom would've approved."

Natty had no use for dresses. And no matter what anybody said, particularly horrible Connie who ran the San Marco Hotel, she thought Sol did just fine raising her. She *liked* wearing pants and playing with boys and going to her father's meetings. But, Natty thought suddenly, maybe her father wasn't happy with her.

"Are you sorry you got stuck with me?" Natty asked him.

Sol looked tenderly at his daughter. "Sorriest thing that ever happened," he teased.

"Hey," Natty said, not sure whether to believe him.

Sol faked a punch at her, and when Natty

raised her hands to protect herself, Sol caught them and laughed gently as he lowered them to her lap.

"Off to bed now," he said, and Natty scampered up to the top bunk. When she heard paper rustling below, she peered over the edge of the bed to see what Sol was up to. He was counting the money in their money box, an anxious look on his face. Natty silently counted with him. They had exactly two dollars and fifteen cents left. Sol needed a job. Badly.

The next morning, Natty and Sol walked purposefully down the stairs to the lobby of the San Marco. The lobby was just as shabby and dark and threadbare as the rest of the building.

Behind the reception desk sat Connie. She not only owned the San Marco, she ran it. Sort of. She sorted mail and collected rent and kept the lobby clean. She hated every minute of it. Years ago, Connie had been a chorus girl. That had been the best time of her life. Now all Connie wanted to do was relive it. Mostly she sat in her room applying makeup, reading movie magazines, and getting fat.

"Morning, Sol," Connie greeted him as he and Natty approached the desk.

"Morning," Sol replied.

Natty didn't say a word. She didn't like Connie, and Connie didn't like her. Natty thought Connie was cheap and rude; Connie thought Natty was a wild, troublemaking street kid.

But Connie liked Sol . . . as much as she liked anyone. She handed him the classified section of the paper. Sol took it gratefully and immediately began skimming the want ads.

"Hey, Sol," said Connie. "Did ya hear about the golfer? Lightning struck his metal shoes and killed him. Shocking, huh?" Connie shook with loud laughter. "Shocking," she repeated with glee.

Natty just glared at her.

Connie's smile faded.

Sol finished looking through the ads by the time he reached the door. He dropped the paper on the front table and left the San Marco, Natty at his heels.

They stepped onto the sagging wooden porch, and Natty commented, "She's disgusting."

"No worse than some," answered Sol mildly.

Sol nodded to the out-of-work men lounging on the hotel steps. They looked lost, as if they'd given up on life, and most of them, Sol reflected, probably *had* given up. But not Sol. Today he was going to look for another job. He was determined to earn a decent salary someday soon. He didn't want to let his daughter down.

Natty and Sol walked through the streets. They passed dilapidated tenement buildings, pawn shops, and saloons. They passed a soup kitchen with a long line of people in tattered clothes waiting for a free meal . . . their only meal of the day. They passed a mother and daughter who had been turned out of their home and were sitting on the curb next to their possessions.

At last they reached Sol's destination. It was the Zeff Employment Agency, but it was really more like a slave market, a place where desperate men gathered, hoping to be offered a job—or at least a day's work. But only a few jobs were posted on the bulletin board outside the office, and many people were waiting for those jobs.

"Same old story," one ragged man with a toothpick in his mouth said hopelessly to Sol.

"Something's going to break. It's got to," Sol replied. He turned to Natty. "Right?"

"Right!"

"See?" Sol said to the man. He winked at Natty. "See you tonight. And stay out of trouble."

"Okay."

Sol watched Natty run down the street. She never waited at the slave market with him. It was boring, and she had plenty of things to do.

"Any more kids back home?" the man with the toothpick asked Sol.

Sol shook his head. "Just me and her."

"No ma?" said the man. "That's tough, huh?"

"That's just how it is," Sol replied with a shrug of his shoulders.

He and the man settled back to wait for something to happen.

Natty made her way through the crowded streets to an alley behind a movie theater, where she met Louie and Frankie. None of them had any money for the movie, so they hung around the back door, which was opened slightly, and sneaked a free look.

"Shh! Someone's coming," whispered Natty suddenly.

Frankie and Louie jumped back and took off down the alley, and Natty turned around. But instead of an usher or a policeman, she found a puppy rummaging through some garbage. He was skinny and flea-bitten, but Natty took one look at his fluffy fur and his big brown eyes and she melted. The puppy needed her.

She picked him up, tucked him inside her jacket, and headed straight for Maxwell Street, with its shoppers and vendors, stalls and push-carts. She walked by people bartering and hawking their wares and arguing over prices. She was looking for her friend Sherman.

After some searching, Natty spotted his pushcart. It was a jumble of pots and pans and clutter, which Sherman sold to make his living. And in the middle of it all was Sherman himself. He was a thin, older man who'd known plenty of hard times but had managed to keep his dignity and his sense of humor.

When Natty approached him, Sherman was in the middle of a sale. A well-dressed woman was examining one of his cooking pots.

"I'm not in the business of giving things away," said Sherman firmly. "This is quality merchandise. Fifteen cents. That's as low as I go. Rock bottom."

The woman hesitated, and Natty saw her chance. "I'll give fifteen cents for it, Mister," she told Sherman with a straight face.

"Wait a minute," exclaimed the woman. "That's my pot, right?"

Sherman looked at Natty as if he were dreadfully apologetic. "Sorry, but she *was* here first," he said to her.

The woman paid Sherman the fifteen cents, took her pot, and left.

Sherman grinned. "Nice move, kid," he said.

Natty crawled under his pushcart to join him inside.

But Sherman's face fell when he saw the

puppy poke his head out of her jacket. "Aw, no," he said.

Natty pulled the puppy out and held him up for Sherman to admire.

"What do I look like?" Sherman asked. "The animal shelter?" More than once, Natty, unable to see an animal suffer, had brought a stray dog or cat for Sherman to take care of.

Natty shrugged. "I'll keep this one."

"Like the last one." Sherman knew better.

"Dad'll let me," Natty said uncertainly. The puppy wriggled happily. "Just look at him."

"But what's it going to be when it grows up?"

"A dog, Sherman."

"You can never tell, kid," Sherman teased. "Could be a lion or something. . . . One of them walruses, maybe."

Natty grinned, nuzzled the puppy, then tucked him back in her jacket and decided to stay a while and help Sherman.

At the slave market, an official stepped out of the office and stood in the doorway, facing the crowd of men waiting outside. A hush fell over them. They looked anxiously up at the official. Sol watched him raise his hand and point to one man in the crowd, then a second, then a third.

"You," he called, "you, and you. Come here."

The three lucky men stepped forward.

Sol stared at the ground, suddenly feeling less optimistic.

But before the official turned his back, he paused. He spotted Sol in the crowd. Sol looked up, and their eyes locked. "Oh, yeah," continued the official. "And you."

Sol entered the office as the first three men left carrying papers. They didn't seem as elated as they had a few minutes before. Sol glared at the official.

"Something wrong?" the official asked sarcastically. He knew Sol, and he thought he was too smart for his own good.

"You're paying those guys half what they're worth," said Sol.

"I didn't hear them complaining."

"They're scared."

"You're a troublemaker, Gann," said the official. "But I got something for you."

The official handed him a paper of his own. Sol read it quickly, then glanced at the other man.

"This says Washington State," Sol exclaimed. "That's clear across country."

"It's steady work, Gann. A real break. Bus leaves today. Six o'clock."

"But I've got a kid," said Sol. "What about my kid?"

"That's not my problem, buddy," replied the

official. "I got one seat on the company bus. Take it or leave it."

Sol stared at the official. How could he take the job? Natty wouldn't be permitted to come with him, and he couldn't leave her behind. But they needed the money badly, and this was a *steady* job, not just a day's work. Steady jobs were scarce.

"Well?" asked the official.

Sol thought again of Natty. At last he dropped the paper on the desk, shaking his head, and turned for the door.

"What are you, nuts?" the official called after him. He couldn't believe that an out-of-work man had turned down one of his jobs. "If you walk out of here, you don't work again. Ever," he threatened. "You in a position to do that, Gann?"

Sol didn't answer. He pushed the door open and looked out at all the listless men waiting for jobs. He put his hand in his pocket and felt the two dollars and fifteen cents—all the money he and Natty had left. Then he drew in a deep breath, took his hat off, and, holding it in his hand, returned to the office.

Sol didn't have a choice. He had to take the job.

Chapter Two

As soon as Sol signed the papers, he dashed out of the office at the slave market to find Natty. It was well into the afternoon, and his bus left at six o'clock. He didn't have much time to find her. He tried to think of the places Natty went most often.

Sol found Louie playing stickball in an empty lot with a group of kids.

"Hey, Louie, you seen Natty?" he shouted to him.

Louie was concentrating on the game. "No," he answered quickly. "Not since this morning."

"You sure?" Sol said. "You know where she is?"

"No idea."

Sol tried a group of Natty's friends who were gathered outside a drugstore. They hadn't seen her either.

Feeling desperate, he ran to Maxwell Street and looked for Sherman's pushcart. When he found Sherman, he told him about the job in Washington and said how important it was for him to find Natty. But Sherman didn't know where she was. She'd left him a couple of hours before.

"She'll turn up," he said, trying to reassure Sol. "She always does."

"In an hour?" asked Sol. "I don't know, Sherman. I just don't know."

"Hey, you got no choice. It's a job."

Sol turned away, feeling panicky. He couldn't search any longer. There would be barely enough time to get to the San Marco and then make the bus.

At the hotel, Sol packed his clothes in a beat-up suitcase. He waited until the very last second before deciding to talk to Connie, then walked slowly down to the lobby, still hoping Natty might turn up. But she didn't.

Sol drew in his breath and knocked on the door to Connie's room.

"Yeah?" she yelled.

"It's Sol. I gotta talk to you."

Connie let Sol in and returned to the blouse she was ironing.

Sol glanced around the room, looking for a place to sit, but it was so crowded with overstuffed furniture and movie magazines and bottles and jars of make-up, that finally he simply stood at one end of the ironing board.

He wiped his sweaty hands on his pants. "Connie, I have to ask a favor. A big one. I've got a job out West at a mill. It's good work. I can't find Natty, though, and the bus to Seattle leaves in an hour."

"Yeah?" said Connie suspiciously.

"Well, I can't take her with me. It's the company bus. I'll have to send for her. As soon as I have the money."

"Yeah?"

"So could you give her this letter? It explains everything. And could you just kind of watch out for her? It won't be that hard, Connie. She's a good kid. Practically takes care of herself. Just make sure she's eating right, getting enough sleep."

"Okay, okay."

"I'll send the money as soon as I can. Then all you have to do is put her on the train." Sol paused, listening, hoping for the sound of Natty coming through the front door.

Connie considered Sol's request. "It'll be extra for taking her to the station. And if you're not paying in advance, it's nine bucks, not seven."

"Sure, Connie. So you'll do it. . . ."

"I'm doing it." Connie was not thrilled with the idea.

Sol nodded. He glanced at the clock on Connie's dresser. It was almost six. He'd have to hustle. "Hey, Connie . . . thanks," he managed to say.

"Yeah, sure." Connie stared after Sol as he hurried out of the room. She was sorry to see him go. But she'd never admit it.

For the second time that day, Sol walked through the streets to the Zeff Employment Agency. He was still hoping to run into Natty. When he finally reached the Lincoln Charters bus, he was the last man to arrive. Even so, he hesitated before he opened the door.

The driver was impatient. "You getting on or not?" he asked.

Sol nodded slowly, then tossed his suitcase onto the rack on top of the bus. A few seconds later he was on his way out of Chicago.

It was dusk by the time Natty returned to the San Marco Hotel, the puppy once again hidden in her jacket. She stood inside the front door, checked to make sure the coast was clear, then rushed through the lobby. She had almost reached the stairs when Connie called to her from behind the reception desk. "Hey, kid! Come here!"

Natty stopped and turned around. Then she walked slowly back to Connie.

"I got something for you," said Connie.

She handed Natty an envelope. "Sol gave it to me before he left."

"Left?" repeated Natty.

"That's right, left. Arrivaderci. Gone." Connie handed Natty the letter, not bothering to tell her anything else.

Natty clutched it in her hand. As she turned away, the puppy yipped loudly.

"What was that?" asked Connie.

"Nothing," replied Natty. She was too confused to make any excuses.

In her room, Natty sank into a chair, the puppy at her feet, and opened the envelope carefully, half afraid to read Sol's note. With a shaky sigh, she unfolded the paper.

"Dear Natty," the note said. "I got a job at a lumber camp in Washington State. They're shipping me out today. I wanted to see you first, but maybe that would've been tougher. You mind Connie. I'll send for you as soon as I can. Love, Dad.

"P.S. This was your mom's. I think you should have it."

Natty shook the envelope, and a small object slid into her hand. It was a folding picture frame. She opened it carefully and found two tiny photos inside, one of Sol and one of her mother not long before she had died.

Natty stared at the picture for a long time, wanting to cry but not allowing the tears to come.

The next few days were difficult ones. Natty had never felt so lost and so alone. Every morning she waited impatiently for the mailman to make his delivery to the San Marco, and every morning he looked through his stack of letters, then shook his head sadly at Natty. Nothing from Sol. So Natty wandered the streets and the railroad yard, thinking and worrying.

Far away, Sol was traveling west on the Lincoln Charters bus. He stared out the window, the autumn leaves whizzing by him in a blur of scarlet and gold, and he thought about Natty. Had Connie given her the letter? Did Natty understand? Was she taking care of herself and staying out of trouble?

One night, Natty grew bored in the little room at the San Marco. She missed Sol. The puppy was whining, and the room shook every time a train rumbled along the el tracks outside the window. Natty decided to take the puppy for a walk.

When she reached the hallway outside Connie's room, she could hear the radio playing, Connie singing along mournfully. Natty took a few steps. Tiptoe, tiptoe, CREAK.

"Where do you think you're going?" Connie appeared in her doorway, her arms folded across her chest.

Natty casually pushed the puppy deeper inside her jacket. "Out," she answered.

"At this hour?"

"Just for a walk."

"Not on your life. Upstairs. That's where you're going, Miss Smarty Pants. Maybe *he* let you run wild, but not me. Understand? It's different with me."

Connie pointed her finger at Natty. "Go on. Get moving."

Natty turned. She stood with her back to Connie. "You're not the boss of me," she cried.

"Bullcrackers! Now move it."

Natty ran up the stairs.

Connie watched her go. "What if he's going to leave her here?" she mumbled. "What if he's never going to send for her?"

The next day, Natty went looking for Sherman. She needed someone to talk to, and Sherman was a patient listener who gave good advice. When Natty reached the pushcart on Maxwell Street, she crawled underneath it, turned a bucket over, and sat on it, her chin resting in her hands.

"You ever ride the rails, Sherman?" she asked.

"What are you thinking about, girl?"

"Nothing."

"Good. 'Cause it's no picnic out there. I saw Fats Chessman get his legs chopped off under the iron wheels. Both of them. Oklahoma Slim got a big scar across his throat. Somebody tried to cut him for his shoes. You can get your guts spilled if you don't know what you're doing. Understand?"

Sherman nodded his head, hoping he'd given Natty a good scare.

Natty sighed. She said goodbye to Sherman and wandered through her neighborhood, the puppy bouncing along at her heels. She was so lost in thought that she didn't notice the angry crowd in the street until she was part of it herself. She looked around. She was standing in front of the apartment building where Frankie lived. A police van was parked nearby.

Natty squirmed her way through the mob of people until she could see what was going on. The crowd booed loudly as a cop led a woman in a faded housedress out of an apartment building. She was followed by five children. The last one, a boy, was carrying the baby.

Natty gasped. The boy was Frankie. His family was being evicted from their home.

Natty wanted to turn and run, but she couldn't take her eyes off the horrible scene. She stood there as two policemen pulled Frankie's father out of the building. And she stood there as several workmen began to carry out the family's belongings and toss them into the street in an untidy pile.

The crowd grew angrier. The people had seen too many evictions. Suddenly, someone had had enough. A rock sailed through the air toward a policeman. The cop struck out with his billy club. Another rock was thrown. And another. Before she knew it, Natty was aiming a rock at one of the cops. She threw it forcefully, feeling the anger build up inside her, anger at Connie, anger at Sol, anger at the world.

She threw another rock.

She bent down to pick up a third—and was grabbed by the arms. Two policemen took hold of her, asked her where she lived, and marched her straight to the San Marco. They pounded on the front door.

"I'm coming, I'm coming," Natty could hear Connie yell from inside. "Hold your horses." The door was yanked open. "Yeah?" said Connie. Her look of annoyance turned to one of astonishment when she saw Natty sandwiched between the burly policemen, the puppy cradled in her arms.

"You responsible for this kid, lady?" asked one of the cops. "Because if you are, the judge'll want to see you in the morning."

Connie rolled her eyes heavenward. Then she pointed at the puppy. "And what is *that?*" she asked.

Natty hung her head. She couldn't think of a thing to say. She knew she was in big trouble. Very big trouble.

And she was right. Connie grabbed her by the shoulder and steered her roughly through the lobby and up the staircase to the room she had shared with Sol.

"I won't stand for any more from you. Hear? I'm drawing the line *right now.*" Connie was shrieking. Natty was sure she could be heard clear across the country. "And that thing," she added, indicating the trembling puppy, "better be gone in the morning."

Connie pushed Natty inside the room and stepped back into the hall. Natty slammed the door behind her. But she'd gone one step too far.

Connie burst back into the room. "You listen to me, twirp. One more thing from you, just one, and I guarantee that you'll be sorry you ever laid eyes on me. I'll make things so hard you'll crawl on your knees begging for mercy. So DON'T PUSH ME!"

Connie left once again. This time, Natty heard the click of a key as Connie locked her door from the outside. Then she heard Connie stomping down the stairs, talking loudly to herself.

"For crying out loud," Connie was saying. "I'm not the kid's mother. I mean, why should I get stuck? Who needs this aggravation?"

Natty didn't waste a second. She pulled a pocket knife from her jeans, stuck it in the lock, and wiggled it around. She tried the door. It opened. Then she crept down the hall and stood at the top of the stairs, listening. All the while, she kept trying to figure out why things were so bad between her and Connie. She didn't know. They just didn't like each other, she guessed. It happened sometimes.

Natty heard Connie on the telephone. "Hello? I want to report an abandoned kid. . . . Yeah, yeah. . . . All alone. You better send somebody right away."

Natty couldn't believe it! An abandoned kid? Who did Connie think she was? Natty dashed back to her room. With shaking hands, she stripped the sheets and blankets off the bunk-beds and knotted them tightly together into two thick ropes. She tied the end of one to the leg of the bed, tossed the other end out the window, put the puppy in a knapsack on her back, and shinnied down the makeshift rope to the edge of the roof. Then she tied the second rope to a storm drain on the roof and slid down into an alley. As soon as her feet touched the ground, she took off at a run.

"Goodbye, San Marco," she thought. "Goodbye, Connie. Thanks for nothing."

Chapter Three

Natty wanted to get out of Chicago as fast as she could, but she had to do one thing first.

She ran to a large barn near Maxwell Street where the vendors stored their pushcarts when they weren't using them. Natty slid open the heavy door and stepped slowly into the shadows. CLUNK! She shrieked as she knocked into a broom, which clattered to the floor. The noise disturbed the bats overhead, and they swooped through the rafters. Natty could hear their wings flapping.

With a shudder, she moved forward again and found Sherman's pushcart in the dark. She pulled the puppy from her jacket and placed him by the cart.

"You stay here," Natty told the puppy as she scratched his ears. She couldn't bring the puppy

with her to find Sol. The trip might be dangerous, and that wouldn't be fair to the puppy.

Natty turned to leave. The puppy leaped up
and started to follow her out of the barn.

Natty sighed.

She picked him up, returned him to the cart,
and tied him to a piece of rope that was
attached to a wheel. "I can't take you. Understand?" she said softly. "I'll miss you, but you
gotta stay with Sherman. He'll take care of
you."

The puppy lay down and rested its chin on its
front paws. It gazed at Natty with sad brown
eyes and whined as she disappeared through the
barn.

Natty ran through the streets, leaving the
puppy behind her. She ran until she reached the
railroad yard. Sherman's words about riding the
rails echoed in her head, but she didn't know
what else to do. She didn't have much money—
not enough for a train ticket to Washington,
anyway—and she had to find Sol.

Natty came to a pile of discarded boxes and
barrels by the railroad tracks. She crept underneath them and looked around from the safety
of her hiding place. Hobos were everywhere.
They hovered in shadows and under empty
cars, waiting for a train to come by. They

looked hard-bitten and tough, and Natty was afraid of them, but she watched them anyway.

As soon as a train roared through the station, the hobos sprinted forward, ran alongside it for a few seconds, and then threw themselves onto the open boxcars.

Now Natty could understand how Sherman's friends had gotten hurt. Still, when the next train came barreling through, Natty found herself darting out of her hiding place, pounding along beside the train, and stretching toward it. She caught hold of a handle and, still running, managed to pull herself partway onto a boxcar—but that was all. She couldn't pull herself any further. The train was traveling too fast.

Natty's legs dangled dangerously over the edge of the car. She looked down and saw the tracks speeding by beneath her so fast that they ran together. The wheels of the train ground out sparks.

She slipped backward. Three hobos in the car watched her. Not one moved. They stared at her with hard, knowing eyes. Natty slipped again, her fingernails clawing along the wooden floor of the car. Just when she thought she would fall under the crushing metal wheels and lose her legs the way Fats Chessman had, a dark figure reached down and grabbed her, hauling her into the car with such force that **she** slammed against the opposite wall.

Natty landed with a bang, gasping for breath. She looked across the car at the person who had saved her. His name was Harry Slade, although Natty didn't know it then. Harry didn't look like the other hobos. He was tough and lean like they were, with a square jaw and penetrating eyes, but he was only sixteen or seventeen years old, and when he spoke his face broke into a warm smile. "You can get hurt that way," he told Natty.

Natty was too shaken up to speak.

"But you didn't," Harry added, still grinning. He winked at her, then moved to the shadows at the far end of the car.

Natty turned to look at the other hobos. They stared back at her.

"Thought you bought the farm," said one.

"Wouldn't have been much left," said another. He snickered.

Natty swallowed the lump that was rising in her throat. She slumped onto the floor, trying to make herself small.

"Leave the kid alone," Harry called out from the shadows.

"Aw, we was just funning," said the first hobo.

Natty looked at Harry. Their eyes met. Then the train grew dark as it pulled away from the lights of Chicago. Natty drew her jacket tightly around her and huddled on the floor of the car.

It was going to be a long night.

Somehow, Natty managed to fall asleep. She didn't awaken until the next morning when the train whistle blew.

She blinked and looked around. The three hobos were gone. Only Harry remained, slouched at the other end of the car, playing an old harmonica.

Natty watched him, listening, enjoying the music. But Harry felt her eyes on him, and he glanced up and abruptly stopped playing, giving her a hard look.

"That was nice," said Natty, trying to smile.

Harry softened. He shrugged, then stuffed the harmonica in his pocket.

Natty glanced around the car again, glad the hobos had left. "Where'd they go?" she asked.

"Nowhere. Anywhere."

Natty nodded. "Where are you going?"

Harry shrugged again. He hadn't given it much thought. "West," he said carelessly.

"Me too," replied Natty. "My dad's out West."

"Yeah?"

"Yeah. In Washington State."

"What part?" asked Harry.

"Uh . . . the middle . . . part."

Harry looked doubtful. "You're running away, huh? On the lam?"

"What makes you say that? I didn't say that."

"You didn't have to," answered Harry.

Natty crossed her arms and turned away.

"You better wise up if you expect to make it," Harry continued.

"I'll do all right, Mr. Know-it-all," snapped Natty.

Harry hid a smile.

Then the whistle blew again, and the train began to slow down. Harry stepped to the edge of the boxcar and swung around so he could see what station they were coming to. Natty followed him, standing behind him in the open door. Harry spoke to her as he watched the scenery fly by. "Don't let the bulls get you," he shouted against the roar of the wind.

"What?"

"Railroad cops."

"You think I don't know that?"

Harry shrugged.

Natty looked down and watched the tracks slide by. She remembered her near miss the night before.

Harry was getting ready to jump. "Bend your knees," he advised Natty. "Roll with it."

"Natch," replied Natty defensively. She was

getting a little tired of Harry and all his help. She wasn't a baby. She could get by.

"Good luck, kid," said Harry.

The whistle blew again.

Harry jumped.

Natty watched him carefully, then took a deep breath—and did just as he'd done. She hit the ground, looked up the track to get her bearings, and saw two railroad cops running toward her, rounding up hobos as they went. Natty turned from them and flung herself down an embankment. When she reached the bottom, she stood up shakily, brushing herself off, and looked around proudly for Harry.

But he was gone. There wasn't a trace of him.

Bewildered, Natty stood where she was, wondering what to do. She hadn't planned to get off at this station. She'd only jumped the train because Harry had gotten off.

Natty wandered along until she came to the station. The sign at the depot said Des Moines. Natty had reached Iowa.

While Natty was escaping from the railroad bulls in Des Moines, Sol was settling into his life as a lumberjack. He and the other men had reached Seattle and had been driven high into the mountains to the lumber mill's Base Camp.

Base Camp looked almost like an army field

camp. It was an elaborate city of white tents. There were sleeping tents, a mess hall, and a mail room. The camp crawled with men. But beyond the confines of the camp stretched an endless panorama of snow-capped mountains and tall fir trees. Sol felt as if he had been taken to the very top of the earth.

At just about the same time that Natty was brushing herself off at the bottom of the embankment, Sol was sitting behind a makeshift desk in one of the sleeping tents. The air was cold, and he was bundled up, his breath coming in white puffs. He bent over a piece of paper, deep in thought, and wrote by the flickering light of a kerosene lamp.

At last he sighed, sat back, and reread the letter he'd just finished. Then he folded it, put it into an envelope, and addressed the envelope to Miss Natty Gann at the San Marco Hotel, Madison Street, in Chicago, Illinois.

Natty waited until evening before approaching the Depot Grill at the Des Moines train station. When she felt that the night was dark enough, she gathered the courage to rummage through the garbage behind the Depot Grill. She was trying to choke down a piece of half-eaten salami that she'd rescued from the slop in a garbage pail, when she noticed a crowd gathering in the shadows of the roundhouse. She stuffed the salami in her jacket and headed toward the roundhouse.

By the time she reached it, she could hear shouting and screaming, like the noise of an angry crowd at a prizefight. Then she realized she could hear growling and snarling, too. Natty stood on her tiptoes at the edge of the crowd, trying to see over the shoulders of the men. Finally she crawled through the forest of legs until she had a good view.

It was a dog fight, except that one of the dogs looked more like a wolf. Natty shuddered. It *was* a wolf, she realized. The men were betting on the fight, and it wouldn't be over until one of the animals was dead.

Natty watched in horror as a Doberman Pinscher and the wolf were unchained. They flew at each other, snarling viciously, their lips curled back. After circling each other warily for several seconds, the wolf leaped at the dog and sank his teeth into his shoulder, gripping him in his powerful jaws. They rolled and growled and fought, but the wolf wouldn't let go. At last, the Doberman fell to the ground, blood spilling out and staining the floor.

Then someone blew a whistle, and the wolf released the dead Doberman as several of the men began to cheer. But an argument broke out in the crowd, and in the midst of it the wolf broke free, leaped up onto a high ledge, then sprang off, sailing over the crowd.

He landed almost on top of Natty, and she gasped in horror. For an instant, their eyes locked, the wolf glaring at her wildly. Then he took off.

A group of the men went after him, led by one named Snake, who was armed with a whip. Natty ran after the men. She paused by the door to the roundhouse and saw that they had cornered the wolf on the far side of the building. Snake was lashing out at the wolf over and over again.

CRACK, CRACK, CRACK.

Natty could almost feel the lashes herself.

But the wolf was not easily beaten. He snarled threateningly, then jumped at Snake, grabbed the whip in his mouth, and knocked him down. He pushed past the group of men and streaked through the roundhouse, dropping the whip as he ran. When he reached the door, he stopped and looked up at Natty. She stared back, then opened the door for him and let him out.

Snake and the men ran after the wolf, shouting angrily. But Natty stepped in their path and pulled the door to the roundhouse shut, blocking them from the wolf. She stared defiantly up at Snake. For an instant he stared back at her. Then he raised his arm and hit her soundly in the face.

Natty fell to the ground.

When she awakened later, her head throbbing, the roundhouse was quiet. Natty pulled herself up and peered out the doorway. The men were gone. The station was deserted.

With a sigh, Natty made her way down the tracks past several rows of waiting boxcars. She found one with a partially opened door and moved over to it cautiously. She paused, listening. Nothing. So she hoisted herself onto the car and waited for her eyes to adjust to the darkness.

So far so good.

Then she became aware of a soft sound that was growing slowly louder. It was the low growl of the wolf. Natty swallowed hard—and the wolf lunged at her, snapping and snarling, from behind some bales of hay that were stacked at the back of the car. His dark ears were laid flat against his head, and his yellow eyes were narrowed to slits.

Natty screamed. She threw herself into a corner of the boxcar and huddled against the walls. The wolf stood poised, ready to spring, and Natty could see blood dripping from his jaws. The blood of the Doberman, thought

Natty. But even as the wolf stood menacingly, threatening Natty's life, she felt sorry for him. He looked as afraid and as proud as he was vicious.

But Natty had to escape. She edged along the wall to the door, the wolf watching her. Then he allowed her to slip outside.

Before Natty found another place to sleep that night, she left a tin of water and the rest of the chunk of salami in the boxcar for the wolf.

Chapter Four

Sol Gann stood in the pouring rain at a pay phone behind a gas station. A truck was waiting nearby.

"Come on . . . come on," Sol was saying impatiently into the phone. A cold rain was drizzling down on him, and he pulled up the collar of his jacket. "Connie? Is that you?" he shouted. "I can hardly hear you. . . . Where's Natty? Did she get my letter? . . . What? . . . I can't hear. Talk louder."

The driver of the truck honked the horn. "Come on, Gann!" he yelled, leaning out the window. "We're waiting on you. Move it." He honked the horn a second time.

Sol motioned for him to wait. Then he turned back to the phone. "She wouldn't just run away, Connie," he said, sounding panicky. "What happened?"

As Sol listened to Connie's explanation, his face grew white. The muscles stood out on his neck. "You're lucky I'm not there, Connie," he said with barely concealed rage. "Because if I was, I'd tear you into little pieces and personally feed you to the river. . . . They *better* find her, Connie. If they don't. . . . Just make sure they do!"

Sol slammed the receiver down and stared furiously at the phone. Then he ran for the truck.

Natty had spent an uncomfortable night in a deserted boxcar at the Des Moines train station. Every so often she would awaken and think about the wolf, wondering if he was all right or if the men had found him and captured him, but she didn't dare go near him.

When the gray light of morning filtered into her hiding place, Natty knew it was time to leave. She hopped onto a freight train that had stopped in the station overnight and soon was on her way west again. This time Natty stayed on the train. A ride was a ride after all. Soon she lost track of how long she'd been traveling. She remembered jumping off the train at some little station in Nebraska, scrounging for food in a garbage can, and getting on board again before the bulls caught her. She remembered being offered half an apple by one unusually nice hobo who rode with her for a while in Colorado.

When the train reached the Rocky Mountains, Natty was awed by the scenery. Around her, the mountains rose up to meet the sky, and streams rushed along, tumbling over waterfalls. The cool weather had turned the leaves of the trees from dull green to blazes of red and orange and crimson. The air smelled clean and seemed so thin that Natty was sure it must be brittle.

Late one day, Natty was riding along inside an enormous cement pipe that was strapped onto an open flatcar. She was enjoying the scenery and idly looking through the junk in her wallet, when suddenly a horrible grinding SCREECH ripped through the air. The train lurched violently, and Natty's wallet flew out of her hands. The cars of the train buckled and swayed, toppling from the tracks. The flatcar smashed onto its side and slid along the ground, the chain that held the cement pipes in place breaking and allowing the pipes to roll away into the woods by the railroad track.

When Natty's pipe came to a stop, she scrambled out and looked up and down the track. She couldn't tell what had caused the wreck, but she could see the train workers pulling themselves from the twisted steel, and smoke and steam rising into the sky.

All at once, not far from Natty, a fuel car exploded, bursting into flame. The train workers began to panic. "She's gonna blow," shouted one. "Look out! Run for it."

Another explosion ripped through the air. Natty ran after the workers but stopped when she caught sight of several bulls rounding up hobos and herding them down the tracks. She couldn't go that way. Out of the corner of her eye she saw something leap from a boxcar and run for the woods. It was the wolf! Natty took off after him.

She crashed through the underbrush, running wildly. When it seemed as if she'd been running for hours, she paused to catch her breath. She looked around, seeing nothing but trees. Where was she?

Behind her, a twig snapped.

Natty jumped. She whirled around—and just missed seeing the two yellow eyes that peered at her through the dense underbrush.

Natty was exhausted. Not knowing what else to do, she sank down to the ground and curled up next to a large, golden-leaved tree for the night.

The next morning, Natty woke up early, just as the sun was rising. She glanced at it briefly to determine which way was west and then began walking in that direction.

It had been a long time since Natty had had anything to eat or drink. She was starving. She tasted some berries, but they were bitter and she spit them out. Later, she caught sight of a stream and ran toward it eagerly. She dropped to her knees on the bank and slurped the water up with her hands, even though it was brackish and slightly green.

She rocked back on her heels, satisfied, and that was when she noticed the paw prints in the mud. They were huge, too big for a dog. Very slowly, Natty looked up.

The wolf was standing over her, poised on a rock on the other side of the stream. Now that Natty could get a good look at him in the daylight, she realized that he wasn't much bigger than a large dog. He had a broad head with dark ears, dark markings around his yellow eyes, and a shiny jet-black nose. Apparently he had cleaned himself up since the fight, because his gray fur was sleek and soft looking. And he had huge feet.

Natty almost giggled—until she noticed the dead rabbit dangling from his mouth. The wolf growled softly at Natty. Then he dropped the rabbit on the rock and disappeared into the woods.

Natty was astonished. Did the wolf really want to help her? She approached the rabbit cautiously, but the wolf was gone. So she found a spot where she could sit down and build a fire. Then she held the rabbit up by its hind legs, suppressing the nausea that rose inside her, and, teeth clenched with determination, began to slit the rabbit's belly with her pocket knife. Soon she was roasting the rabbit on a crude spit over a fire and enjoying her first real meal in several days.

She was almost finished when the storm blew in. A drenching rain poured down on her without warning, dousing the fire. Natty shivered in her light jacket and looked around desperately for some sort of shelter. Ahead of her were cliffs with overhanging rocks. She ran toward them as lightning crackled and thunder roared. By the time she reached them, she was soaked by the bone-chilling rain. She came to a small cave, crawled inside, and collapsed on the rock floor.

She had barely caught her breath when she heard the familiar low growl. She swung around, her eyes searching the dim cave.

The wolf was backed up against the far wall. He looked wet and bedraggled now, very different from the proud animal that had offered her the rabbit not long ago. But his snarl was menacing. Natty edged toward the entrance to the cave. She looked out at the pouring rain. All at once she was too tired to run away again. She didn't care what happened to her. She huddled against a wall, curled herself into a tight ball, and fell asleep.

The storm raged during the night, but when morning arrived the sky was clear and blue, and the sun lit the brilliant leaves and the stark white of the birch trees.

Natty stirred, realizing she was sleeping comfortably for the first time in days. She seemed to have a warm pillow under her head. Natty patted it—and awoke with a start. The wolf! He was curled up with her, watching her contentedly, and Natty had laid her head on the soft fur of his back.

Natty patted him, and he moaned happily. She had found a friend.

After that, Natty and the wolf traveled together. Natty had to scramble along to keep up with the wolf's fast trot. He would run ahead of her, wait impatiently for her to catch up, then run ahead again.

The wolf was always wary, always on the alert, watching out for himself and for Natty. Once, when they had stopped to drink from a stream of clear water, the wolf sniffed the air, and the fur on the back of his neck stood on end. He looked behind them. Natty put her hand on his back.

"What is it?" she asked him.

The wolf whined an answer.

Natty followed his gaze, and through the underbrush she saw a farmhouse.

That meant people!

"Okay!" cried Natty. She jumped to her feet and ran toward the clearing.

But when she turned to find the wolf, he had disappeared. . . .

Chapter Five

Natty was so relieved to find a safe place and the possibility of some good food that she didn't waste any time looking for the wolf, even though she was sorry he had left her.

She raced to the clearing, then slowed down and approached the house slowly. The little farm looked makeshift and poor, the buildings rough-hewn, almost ramshackle. The house was built from logs, and the sagging outbuildings leaned in all directions. A tired old mule that looked as if it were on its last legs nodded to Natty from the barn door. Several scrawny chickens clucked nervously in the henhouse.

Natty hesitated, then banged on the door. Al, a farmer with a hard, chiseled face, opened it a crack and peeped out. Natty could just make out the rifle at his side.

She gulped. "Morning. . . ."

Al stared at her. "What do you want? You alone?" he asked. He glanced over her shoulder, checking the woods. He didn't want any hobos getting the idea that they would be fed here. He and his wife barely had enough for themselves.

Natty looked to the woods too, and was disappointed to see that there was still no trace of the wolf. "Yeah, I guess so," she said, turning back to Al. "I'm lost."

Al's wife appeared beside him at the door. Her name was Rosie. She was young and looked much kinder and more open than her husband. But she was very plain. Hard work and hard times had taken their toll on her. Natty could see that she was going to have a baby soon.

"Come on in," Rosie said. She led Natty to the kitchen, sat her at a rough wooden table, and placed a huge plate of food in front of her. She sat at the table and chatted with Natty while she ate, but Al crossed his arms and leaned against the wall, scowling.

"It must have been pretty scary out there," Rosie commented as Natty ate. "All by yourself."

"I had a friend," said Natty, her mouth full of food.

Al glared at her suspiciously. "Who?" he demanded. He knew there were hobos in the woods, he just knew it. He didn't trust Natty for a second.

Natty paused. "A wolf," she said finally.

Al shook his head and stalked over to the screen door. He pushed through it, letting it slam behind him. A wolf, of all things. It would be after his livestock in no time flat. Al decided he would have to be on the lookout.

Natty watched him bang out of the house. "I think I better be going," she said.

"Nonsense. Don't mind him," said Rosie.

"I don't think he likes me."

"Don't take it personal. It's not you. It's these times. They're changing him. He'll be all right again when things turn better."

"When's that going to be?" asked Natty. She wanted things to turn better *fast*.

But Rosie just smiled and shrugged.

Natty earned her food by helping Al and Rosie work their field. Natty hoed, and Al walked behind the plow, pushing it through the soil. Rosie drove the mule. Natty was surprised that she had to do such hard work, considering she was pregnant, but, like Rosie had said, it was the times.

When an eerie howl from the woods surrounding the field sliced through the air, Natty paused and grinned. It was the wolf, of course. She whistled back to him.

But Al looked up angrily. The wolf was the enemy.

"Haw, Bucky! Pull," called Rosie, and Natty and Al returned to work, but Natty kept one eye on the woods.

The sun beamed down on the fields. Natty was hot and sweaty. She stopped to mop her forehead and noticed that Rosie had stopped, too. She was swaying slightly. Then her knees buckled, and she fell to the ground.

Al dropped the plow and ran to her. Quickly, he lifted her in his arms and ran toward the house.

"What's wrong?" called Natty, worried.

"Get the mule," was all Al would say.

"Is she okay?"

"Get the mule!"

Natty ran after the mule and caught its reins. She walked it back to the farmyard for Al.

Later, when Al had returned to the fields, Natty poked her head into Rosie and Al's room. Rosie was lying weakly on the bed, propped up against pillows. She smiled when she saw Natty.

"You all right?" Natty asked, stepping inside.

"I'm fine."

Natty looked doubtful. "Yeah?"

"Uh huh. Come here," said Rosie, patting her bulging stomach. "It's moving. Feel it."

Natty wrinkled her nose. "Nah . . ."

"Don't be scared," Rosie said with a smile.

Natty stood by the bedside. Rosie took Natty's hand and placed it on her belly.

Natty's eyes widened as she felt the baby kick. "Is that it? Is that the baby?"

"That's his foot."

"It must hurt. Getting kicked like that," Natty said.

"No. The losing hurts, but not the bearing. We had another one that died."

"My momma died when I was a kid. I hardly remember her." Natty pulled the picture frame from her pocket. She opened it and held it out toward Rosie. "There. That's her. She was pretty, huh?"

"Real pretty," said Rosie.

"I look like my dad," Natty went on. "He's in Washington. Where I'm going."

"Does he know you're coming?" Rosie asked.

"More or less." Natty wandered over to the window and gazed out. "He was going to send for me, but I couldn't wait."

"You can stay here," Rosie offered.

Natty turned around, surprised.

"It'd be a help to me."

"What about him?" asked Natty.

"Al? Don't you worry about him. We'll win him over." She winked at Natty.

Natty spent that night in a shed at the farm. She hadn't slept in a bed in a long time, and even though this makeshift one was a far cry from the top bunk in her room at the San Marco, it was better than a cave or a boxcar, and Natty snuggled deep under the covers, dreaming happily.

But early the next morning, she was awakened by a commotion in the farmyard. She could hear yips and growls. In the henhouse, the chickens squawked wildly. Then Natty heard a gun go off.

In a flash, she was out of bed and running into the yard. She reached the henhouse just in time to see three coyotes streaking toward the woods. The wolf was after them. He was trying to keep them from the chickens, but Al would never believe it.

And that was when Natty noticed Al, his gun aimed at the wolf's head.

"RUN!" she screamed to the wolf. Then she leaped onto Al just as he was pulling the trigger. The gun fired harmlessly into the air.

Al glared furiously at Natty. Without pausing to think, Natty went after the wolf, running across the fields, leaving the farm behind her.

Rosie watched from the porch. She shook her head slightly, then rubbed her belly protectively. "You'll always have a home," she whispered to the baby. "You'll never be on your own. I promise."

Across the country, in the state of Washington, Sol was trying to work at the mill and search for Natty at the same time. He was desperate to find her, but he was pretty sure she was still in Chicago, probably not too far from the San Marco.

He decided to start his search by calling Connie again, and his boss let him use the phone in the office.

"Listen hard, Connie," Sol was saying. He put his hand over his ear to block the noise of the men in the background. "I'm coming back there to find her myself. The boss gave me a week. . . . What do you mean, sit down? I don't have to sit down. Just tell me what's going on."

But as Sol listened to what Connie had to tell him, he realized he did need to sit down. He sank slowly into a chair. "Where?" he whispered. He listened for a few seconds. "Yeah . . . yeah." He dropped the phone back into the cradle without saying goodbye. Then he stared blankly at the walls of the mill office.

"What's the matter, Gann?" asked his boss.

"They found my kid's wallet. Buried under a train. In Colorado."

"Aw, jeez . . ."

"What on earth was she doing in Colorado?" Sol wondered.

Chapter Six

Natty and the wolf, together again, walked for miles, Natty holding onto the ruff of fur around the wolf's neck. They walked until they reached a little town in Colorado called Chugwater. It was hardly a town, though, just a stark collection of houses, a couple of stores, a gas station, and a church stuck out in the middle of nowhere, surrounded by mile after mile of rolling hills and fields that were ready to be harvested.

Although the wolf looked as if he'd much rather stay in the woods, Natty walked resolutely up what there was of Main Street, and the wolf followed. She stopped in front of a grocery store, her stomach grumbling. Maybe she could work for some food, the way she had done at the farm.

"Hey, Mister," she said, approaching the clerk who was arranging vegetables in the stand in front of the store. "I wonder if you could let me—"

"No!" exclaimed the clerk, not waiting for Natty to finish her sentence. "I'm sick of you kids panhandling. You hear me? Now beat it!"

Natty backed out of the store and started up Main Street again, only to find a group of teenaged boys blocking her path. They were lounging all over the sidewalk, looking lazy but tough.

"Wrong. All wrong," the leader, Parker, said to Natty. He nodded toward the store she'd been in.

"Huh?"

"Your line. The way you hit on him."

"You know a better way?"

"You'd be surprised," spoke up Leon, standing behind Parker with a knowing smirk on his face.

Natty looked at him. He was thin and dressed in raggedy clothes. "Not by you, Ringworm," she said to him.

"Hey, you're asking for it." Leon moved forward threateningly.

But the wolf was much more threatening as he stepped in front of Natty and snarled at Leon.

Leon jumped back.

"Nice dog," commented Parker, forcing a smile.

"He's a wolf," replied Natty coldly.

"Oh yeah? A wolf. Ha ha! There's a bounty on wolves around here. Too bad."

"What're you talking about?"

"They shoot wolves, stupid," said Leon.

Natty tightened her grip on the wolf. "Don't call me stupid," she shot back.

"Take it easy, girl," Parker said smoothly. "We're not the enemy. Maybe we can help."

"How?" Natty challenged him.

"The stem's tough. Especially on your own."

"The stem?" repeated Natty. "What's that mean?"

"Cripes," said Leon, witheringly. "The girl's green."

"Begging," Parker explained. "Working the street. It's hard. But we got other ways. There's a group of us tramping together. . . . You hungry?"

Natty shrugged her shoulders. "Maybe."

Parker smiled. He was sure Natty was starving. He motioned for her to follow him as he and the other boys disappeared into an alley.

Parker led Natty to an abandoned building on the outskirts of the town. If Natty had thought Al and Rosie's farm was ramshackle, then she decided she hadn't known the meaning of the word. Parker's place seemed to be crumbling before her very eyes. Inside, it was furnished with crates and boxes and broken chairs. It was dim, lit only by firelight and a couple of candles. There was no running water or electricity. Natty couldn't even tell what the building had been before Parker and his gang had taken it over. She wondered how long Parker and the others had been living there—and what had happened to their families. But she didn't ask any questions.

The first thing Parker did was give Natty a plate of stew. She ate it hungrily, the wolf by her side, and looked around. Aside from Parker and Leon and the other boys, Franco, Rusty, and Davey, there was one girl, Annie, who slouched against Parker and stared sullenly at Natty.

"So you're looking for your old man, huh?" Parker asked Natty. He smiled charmingly at her.

Natty nodded. "He's waiting for me."

"Yeah, sure," said Leon. "And my name's Franklin D. Roosevelt."

The others laughed. Natty dropped her eyes and went back to her stew.

"I haven't seen my old man in three years," said Franco. "He took off. It killed him, watching my old lady make one potato go seven ways."

Natty finished her stew, and Parker said, "Get her some more, Annie."

"But we don't—"

"Get some, Annie."

Annie grimaced, then refilled Natty's bowl from a pot of stew cooking in the remains of a fireplace.

Davey spoke up. "Towards the end, my old man couldn't even look at us. That's why he left. I don't blame him."

"Hey," said Leon. "All *mine* did was beat on me and my old lady anyway. I was glad when he left."

"They all think they're coming back," said Rusty softly. "But once they're gone, they figure out they're better off."

"And so's everybody else," said Parker.

The stew Natty had eaten began to feel like ice cubes in the pit of her stomach. She looked anxiously from Rusty to Parker. Sol hadn't abandoned her. He wouldn't do that . . . would he?

"Well, we don't need them anymore," Parker suddenly said proudly. "We've got each other. We're like our own family. The difference is, with us you get to pick your relatives. And everybody carries their share."

Natty thought that over. She knew exactly what Parker was doing. He wanted her to stay with the kids and help them with their tramping and food stealing and whatever else they did.

And Natty was tempted. After all, Sol *had* gone off without her.

So Natty stayed with the kids . . . until Sunday. That was the day Parker wanted to steal the bull so he could sell it to earn money for food. He chose Sunday morning because most of the people in Chugwater were attending church then. No one would be around.

Parker and the kids ran with Natty and the wolf to a field just outside of town. And there, penned up by himself, was a black Angus bull. An *enormous* black Angus bull. The kids clustered around the loading chute that led to the bull's pen, talking in whispers, looking around furtively.

Parker pointed to the bull. "That's him. Ready?"

Natty hesitated. "I don't know. . . ."

"What?" snapped Parker.

"It's stealing."

"Not the way I see it. The rich just keep getting richer. But what do the poor get? Nothing. Now, if you're with us, you chip in like everybody else. If not, get lost."

"She's just yellow," said Leon.

"I am not!"

"Then shut up and let's go." Parker strode away, daring Natty to follow.

Natty wasn't scared. She had to prove that to

them. So, swallowing hard, she ran across the field after Parker.

On the other side of the pen was parked a truck with a trailer attached to it. Leon, Franco, and Annie were in charge of the truck. They released the handbrake and silently rolled the truck along until the trailer was standing at the end of the loading chute.

Parker, Davey, Rusty, Natty, and the wolf stood at the pen, looking in at the bull. It pawed the ground and snorted menacingly.

Parker ignored this. "We get him in the trailer and we're off. It's easy."

"Yeah, easy," said Davey uncertainly.

"A snatch," said Rusty. He and Davey exchanged a look.

"Okay," Parker said, turning to Natty. "You push him from behind." He turned to Rusty and Davey. "You guys get the gate."

"Where are you going to be?" asked Natty.

"I'm the driver. Okay? I mean, you don't mind, do you?"

Natty shrugged. But how come she was the one who had to get in the pen with the bull?

Parker nodded to the boys. They opened the gate at the end of the chute.

Very slowly, Natty climbed over the fence and jumped down inside the pen. She took a few steps forward. Then the wolf sailed over the fence and landed at her side. He wouldn't let her face the bull alone. Natty hung onto him for dear life.

"Okay, bull. Go on. Shoo," said Natty, advancing as if she were walking on eggs. "Pssst. Go on." *I must be crazy,* she thought.

The bull stamped his feet. He snorted at Natty. Natty gulped.

"Remember," Parker called encouragingly from the fence. "He's more scared of you than you are of him."

"Want to bet?" said Natty.

Suddenly, the wolf stepped between Natty and the bull. He crouched down, ready to spring, and inched forward in slow motion.

The next thing Natty knew, the bull turned calmly and ambled down the chute into the trailer! Leon, Franco, and Annie closed the trailer's tailgate. Then they began jumping up and down, congratulating each other. Natty hugged the wolf hard.

Parker patted Natty on the back, but she shrugged away. She was not proud of what she had done. She glared at Parker as he climbed into the cab of the truck with Annie. He turned the key in the ignition, and the engine roared to life. Then he put the truck in gear, but the only thing that happened was that the back wheels spun wildly, throwing gravel into the air.

"You know how to drive this thing?" asked Natty.

"Hey, get off my back," said Parker irritably. "Push. All of you."

The kids gathered behind the truck and pushed. The wheels continued to spin, but the truck didn't move. The kids rocked it up and down. Nothing.

Inside the trailer, the bull began to stamp and bellow loudly. Someone was bound to hear him, Natty thought.

And sure enough. . . . "Uh oh," said Leon.

The kids turned. A caretaker was zooming toward them on his motorcycle, rifle in hand.

"Get us out of here, will you?" cried Franco.

"What do you think I'm trying to do?" Parker gripped the gearshift and jerked it back and forth.

"I thought you said everyone was in church," said Natty accusingly.

"I was wrong," Parker replied.

At that moment, the wolf took off down the road toward the caretaker. Natty called after him, panicking.

Parker gunned the engine one last time, and the truck lurched forward. As it picked up speed, Leon and Franco jumped into the cab, and Davey and Rusty leaped onto the running boards. But Natty ran down the road, calling for the wolf.

Finally, he turned around and began loping

toward her. Natty made a dash for the truck. "Wait for us!" she yelled.

She ran behind the truck, grabbing the rear bumper as if she were trying to haul herself onto a boxcar, but she was too late. She couldn't get a grip on the bumper, and she fell to the ground as the truck sped away.

When she looked up, the caretaker was looming over her.

Chapter Seven

The caretaker turned Natty and the wolf over to the police, and the police turned them over to an uninviting place called the Greely Industrial School. They didn't arrive until that night, but even in the dark Natty could see that it was a huge, gloomy brick building surrounded by a tall chainlink fence—with a gate that locked.

A guard met Natty at the entrance to the school and helped her out of the van that had picked her up at the police station. Natty snapped her fingers, and the wolf started to jump down after her, but the guard put his arm out, barring the wolf's way.

"Hey," said Natty.

"No pets," said the guard firmly.

"But—"

"Sorry, kid."

"What are you going to do with him?" Natty cried, her voice becoming shrill.

"We'll take care of him."

The wolf growled softly as the guard slammed the van door shut, cutting him off from Natty. Natty could see the wolf cock his head at her in confusion and then snarl as he realized what was happening.

The van drove off into the darkness. Natty had no idea where it was going.

"The wolf and I," said Natty, swallowing back tears, "we're traveling together."

"Sorry," the guard repeated. And then he wouldn't say any more.

He led Natty to the office of Sam Parks, one of the directors of the school. Mr. Parks shuffled through the papers on his desk, looking extremely annoyed.

"Okay," he said. "Let's make this fast. Here we go. Name?" he asked, selecting a form.

"Natty Gann," Natty replied softly.

"Full name. Speak up."

"Natalie Sue Gann."

"Where do you live?"

"Uh . . ."

"Vagrant. Where's your folks?"

"I, uh . . . I'm looking for my . . ."

"Orphan," snapped Sam.

"I'm not," said Natty.

Mr. Parks turned to the guard. "Put her in 1, Jake."

"I'm no orphan!" Natty shouted over her shoulder as Jake led her away.

"Yeah, sure kid, sure," replied Mr. Parks.

Jake and Natty were met by a tough-looking matron who took Natty to the girls' wing, gave her an itchy, white regulation nightgown to change into, and then guided her through a dreary dormitory with cement walls. The only furniture in the room were two rows of metal beds.

The room was dark, and the girls in the beds were supposed to be asleep, but Natty knew they weren't. She could feel them staring at her.

The matron stopped by an empty bed. "This is yours," she informed Natty. "No talking after eight. Up at five." She turned on her heel and left, calling one more "No talking!" over her shoulder. A few seconds later, a door slammed, and Natty heard a deadbolt slide into place.

Locked in.

Natty lay down on the hard mattress. She was scared of the matron and scared of the school and even scared of the other girls, but all she could think about was the wolf. Where was he? What were they going to do with him . . . or to him?

She was lying there worrying when Twinkie, a girl in one of the beds nearby, climbed out and tiptoed over to Natty. "Welcome to the funny farm," she said. "What are you in for?"

"Cattle rustling," answered Natty.

"No joke?" Twinkie giggled.

"Shh!" whispered another girl.

Twinkie ignored her. She smiled at Natty. "You're lucky you got this bed. It was June's. She's stuck in solitary. We may never see her again. She tried to break out. Dumb."

The matron's voice boomed through the darkness. "QUIET!"

Twinkie shrugged and darted back to her bed. Natty stared out the barred windows of the dormitory.

Wolf, where are you? she thought. And then, *Dad, where are you?*

At that moment, Sol was nearer than Natty would ever have believed. He was in Colorado, at the site of the train wreck. That very afternoon he had sat across a desk from an apologetic railroad official who had handed over Natty's battered wallet.

"We were gonna send it on," the official told Sol, "but the lady said keep it, so we just hung on to it."

Connie, thought Sol. She was probably glad to have Natty out of her hair.

The official drove Sol to the mountain where the crash had occurred. Sol didn't even notice the sunlight filtering through the autumn leaves or the mist that hid the snowy mountaintops. He kept his eyes glued to the ground as he turned papers and broken glass and dented metal over with his foot, hoping for some clue that would tell him what had happened to his daughter.

When he thought he had searched everywhere, he started over again.

"They went through this area with a fine-tooth comb," said the official. "Didn't find nothing."

Sol set his jaw. "Maybe she wasn't even *on* your train. Maybe somebody stole her wallet." He glared at the official, then returned to his search.

At the Greely Industrial School, Natty and Twinkie were bending and stretching in the exercise yard. Rita, the exercise matron whom Twinkie called Rita the Rhino, stood before the rows of girls, barking out orders.

Twinkie whispered something loudly to Natty.

"Okay, Twinkie," shouted Rita. "Fifteen laps. In silence. . . . And take your friend," she added, pointing at Natty. "The rest of you fall out."

Twinkie groaned. She and Natty began jogging around the yard as the other girls went inside. They had run two laps when Natty heard a familiar howl. She scanned the area frantically, searching for the wolf. At first she saw nothing; then she noticed the truck with CHARLIE LINFIELD—BLACKSMITH painted on its side. Two guards were dragging the wolf toward the truck, a wire muzzle binding his nose and mouth and a rope looped around his neck. The wolf whined and struggled. He twisted and turned, thrashing and leaping in the air. The guards could barely control him.

Natty stopped jogging and ran to the fence that barred her from the wolf. She clung to it breathlessly, unable to move.

"You're asking for it," Twinkie warned her as she ran by.

"Keep moving, sister!" Rita yelled.

"I told you," called Twinkie.

But Natty didn't pay attention to either of them. She couldn't take her eyes off the wolf. The guards managed to force him inside a small cage. Then they handed him over to the blacksmith, and one of them said, "He's all yours, Charlie. And good riddance."

The cage was lifted into Charlie's truck. Natty saw the wolf crouching indignantly inside, hatred in his eyes. Then she saw the gunrack in the back of the truck.

"NO!" screamed Natty. "Don't hurt him! Let him go."

But the van drove off, and Rita grabbed Natty's shoulder and pulled her away from the fence. Then she marched Natty off to the isolation cells.

SLAM! The door clanged shut as Rita pushed Natty inside one of the cells, then turned crisply and strode back through the cold, damp corridor, her footsteps echoing behind her.

Natty looked around her cell. It was tiny, with barely enough room for a cot. There were no windows, just a slit in the heavy metal door. And it was cold. The floor and walls were cement.

After Rita left, Natty sank slowly to the floor, huddling in the corner, tears finally spilling down her cheeks. Of all the terrifying things that had happened since Sol left her—escaping from Chicago, the fight at the depot in Des Moines, the train wreck—surely this was the worst.

Natty's stay in the cell left her quieter, but more determined than ever to find Sol—and the wolf.

The first evening she was out of isolation, she ran into Twinkie as the girls trooped upstairs after dinner.

"You okay?" Twinkie asked.

"I'm getting out of here, Twinkie," Natty said grimly.

"Me too," replied Twinkie. "Three years, five months, and seventeen days."

"I can't wait that long."

Twinkie rolled her eyes. "Forget it, would you?" She knew what happened when kids tried to escape from Greely. But she didn't know Natty.

Natty wasn't about to forget it. She'd already worked out her escape. She'd had plenty of time to plan it while she was in the isolation cell.

Later that evening, Natty, tiptoeing, led Twinkie to the shower room to show her how she intended to get away from Greely. She peered through the barred window, then pointed her finger. "That one," she told Twinkie.

Twinkie looked at the car Natty was pointing to in the parking lot below. She couldn't believe Natty's choice. "Oh no," she said nervously. "It's the Rhino's."

Rita's car? Natty shrugged. She hadn't known it was hers, but she didn't care. She was going to escape and save the wolf. That was all there was to it. And Rita's car was perfect for her plan. It had a rumble seat.

Natty and Twinkie turned to find the matron

glaring at them from the doorway. They beat a hasty retreat to their beds. The matron followed them, then stood in the dormitory, taking a quick head count. When she was finished, she flicked off the light.

"No talking!" she roared as she left the room.

As soon as Natty heard the door lock at the end of the hall, she threw back her covers and pulled off her nightshirt. Underneath she was fully dressed. She stuffed the nightshirt under the blanket, trying to make the bed appear as if she were still sleeping in it, and crept through the dormitory to the bathroom.

On the wall between two of the sinks was a small metal screen that covered the heating ducts. Natty pried off the wire mesh.

A shadow fell across the wall.

Natty jumped and turned around guiltily.

It was only Twinkie. "You're not gonna squeal, are you?" Natty asked.

In answer, Twinkie pulled a hat from behind her back and held it out. "Here. Take this. It's mine. Maybe they won't recognize you."

Smiling, Natty took the hat and squeezed through the opening. She could hear Twinkie replacing the wire grating behind her and scurrying back to the dorm. Then Natty began inching through the ducts to the boiler room, being as quiet as possible.

In the boiler room, she paused and listened. She heard nothing. Good. She looked around and could just make out the coal chute. That was the last part of her escape route.

A few seconds later, sooty but very pleased with herself, Natty emerged in the yard of the Greely Industrial School. She made her way silently toward the parking lot, staying in the shadows, avoiding the guards. When she reached Rita's Ford coupe, she didn't hesitate a second. She opened the rumble seat on the back of the car, slipped inside, and closed it after her.

Then she waited.

After a while, the Rhino climbed into her car and drove off. She had just reached the gate when lights blinked on in the girls' dormitory and an alarm bell began ringing loudly.

But Rita didn't stop. She drove through the gates and along a country road to a spot at the edge of Chugwater called the OK Cafe. Then she parked the car and got out, slamming the door behind her.

Natty stayed hidden, listening until she was sure Rita was inside. Then, with Twinkie's hat pulled low over her eyes, she scrambled out of the rumble seat. A couple was walking through the parking lot. Natty walked up to them boldly and asked as politely as she knew how if they could please tell her the way to Charlie Linfield's.

The man smiled and pointed down the road. "About a half a mile in that direction."

"Thanks, mister," she replied.

Natty walked off, grinning. She had escaped again.

Chapter Eight

Although Natty was glad she wasn't far from Charlie Linfield's, she began to feel apprehensive. The closer she got to Charlie's, the worse she felt. What if the wolf wasn't there? What did Charlie want with him anyway? What if Charlie had—? But Natty couldn't think about that. She kept on going, jogging down the lonely road.

Charlie's home was a log cabin in a wooded area. It was dimly lit and looked frightening to Natty, but she crept past it anyway, into the barn behind the house. And there was Charlie, hammering away at a huge forge next to a blazing furnace.

Natty swallowed hard. Then she sneaked over to Charlie's truck, which was parked in the barn, and peeped inside. There was the cage the guards had put the wolf in, but it was empty.

Natty looked around and saw a shovel leaning against the wall. She reached for it and silently raised it above her head. Then she snuck up behind Charlie.

"Where's the wolf?" she screamed.

Charlie jumped with surprise. He lunged toward Natty, aiming a red-hot poker straight at her. Then he saw that his intruder was just a kid. "Who are you?" he asked gruffly.

He advanced on Natty, but she held her ground. She was about to answer him when Charlie stepped into a shaft of light, and for the first time Natty could see his face clearly. It was a horrible mass of scars, pocked and pitted and stretched, the right side pulled back in a permanent grimace. Natty drew in her breath sharply. Then she continued. "If you've done anything to him . . ."

"You'll what?" countered Charlie.

"Where is he?"

"Why?"

"He's mine."

"Wolves ain't nobody's. He belongs out there." Charlie nodded toward the woods.

"You let him go?" Natty asked. She didn't know whether to be happy or sad.

"I didn't eat him." Charlie left the barn and crossed the yard. Natty followed him cautiously, the shovel still raised. Charlie opened the door to a shed at the back of the cabin.

Out bounded the wolf! He leaped joyfully at Natty.

"I wouldn't kill him," said Charlie. "I knew he belonged to somebody. I was just waiting to see what happened."

Natty dropped the shovel and sank to her knees, burying her head in the fur around the wolf's neck. She hugged him and hugged him, not wanting to let go.

She had found her friend again.

Charlie let Natty and the wolf spend the night at his place. Early the next morning, they sat companionably together on the porch, enjoying the stillness of dawn. Natty was surprised at what a gentle man Charlie had turned out to be. He loved animals, all animals, and as they sat a deer wandered into the clearing, knowing it could eat there safely. A squirrel ran onto the porch and scurried away with some nuts Charlie had put out. Even the wolf liked Charlie. He lay at Natty's side, relaxed and peaceful.

Charlie broke the silence by saying simply, "They'll be looking for you."

"I know," replied Natty.

"You could turn yourself in."

Natty shook her head. "I'm going to Seattle. I've got to."

Charlie understood. "I'll give you a ride to

River Bend," he offered. "At least it's a start."

Natty smiled. Charlie was okay.

If Natty had known where Sol was, though, she might not have smiled. He had given up searching for clues at the site of the train wreck and was heading west on a train called the *Rocky Island,* going back to Seattle.

The train rumbled slowly through the Rocky Mountains that Natty had liked so much. The next stop was River Bend. But Sol thought Natty was dead, and Natty thought Sol was in Seattle. They would both be at the River Bend depot together for several moments—Sol on the train, Natty just outside the station—and they would never know it.

When Charlie dropped Natty off at the depot, he handed her a leather satchel. "There's food in here," he told her. "And money for a ticket."

"No, Charlie." Natty couldn't take money from Charlie.

"Don't tell me no. Just take it." He smiled crookedly.

So Natty accepted the satchel, then leaned back into the truck to kiss Charlie on his scarred cheek.

"Go on. Get out of here," said Charlie. He

glanced at the wolf. "Wolf, you watch out for her, you hear?" Charlie watched Natty and the wolf cross the street. Then he drove away quickly.

Natty entered the small one-room train station, the wolf walking anxiously at her side. He didn't like being inside buildings, even with Natty.

Natty stepped up to the man behind the ticket counter. "How much to Seattle?" she asked.

The clerk peered at her, his glasses sliding down his nose. "On the *Rocky Island?* Ten dollars and fifty cents."

As Natty counted out the money, the wolf jumped up on his hind legs and thrust his huge front paws on the counter. He growled protectively.

The clerk leaped back. "Hey!"

"He's okay," said Natty.

"Well, get him off my counter."

Natty snapped her fingers at the wolf, and he sat down.

But the clerk was staring at Natty. "Wait here," he said suddenly. He disappeared behind a partition.

When he was out of Natty's sight, he picked up a phone, dialed, and began whispering urgently into it. "It's Hector at the depot," he said. "That girl you're looking for? I got her."

But when he returned to the ticket window, the station was empty except for Twinkie's hat.

Natty wasn't taking any chances. She had thought there was something funny about the clerk's behavior, and she had run from the depot and disappeared into the woods . . . just as the *Rocky Island* pulled into the station.

If she could have seen the train, she would have noticed a tired-looking man staring vacantly out one of the windows.

It was Sol.

Chapter Nine

Natty and the wolf trudged along the edge of a deserted highway. It was a cool autumn day, and Natty stuffed one hand into her pocket and held on to the wolf's warm ruff with her other hand. The countryside was bleak, even in the sunshine, but Natty didn't care. She was glad to be leaving Greely Industrial School and River Bend behind. She decided she would miss Charlie and Twinkie, but no one else. Mostly she was just glad to be with the wolf again.

Natty walked and daydreamed, stopped to rest, then walked some more. When the wolf turned and peered over his shoulder, hackles raised, snarling softly, Natty looked down the road, too. At first she saw nothing. Then an old Ford truck rolled into view. Natty stuck her thumb out. She figured she was owed a ride, since she'd lost her money and missed out on the *Rocky Island*.

The driver slowed to a stop when he saw Natty. He rolled down the window. "Hi there. Need a lift?" he asked pleasantly.

He was a middle-aged man with a friendly face and an easy grin, but his smile faded when he saw the wolf. He glared at him as the wolf curled his lips back, the snarls growing louder. "What about him?" he asked.

"He won't be any trouble. Honest," said Natty. She wasn't about to miss out on a perfectly good ride.

The driver shrugged, then leaned over to open the passenger door for Natty, but he wouldn't let the wolf in. "He rides in back," he said, pointing over his shoulder. He walked around and opened the tailgate. Natty went with him. She snapped her fingers, and the wolf reluctantly jumped into the open area behind the truck's cab. As soon as Natty and the driver were settled in the front, the wolf paced over to the rear window of the cab and watched them tensely.

"Name's Buzz," said the driver after they'd traveled several miles. "That's a fine-looking animal. I could use a strong thing like that. I have a big yard where I keep my trucks. Had one stolen about a month ago. I'd like to have a watchdog. Would you be interested in selling him?"

Natty laughed. Sell the wolf? "No," she said. "I don't think so."

"You sure?" asked Buzz. "Cash on the line. I bet you could use it where you're going."

"I can't sell him," said Natty. "I don't even own him."

"Who does?"

"Nobody. He's not like that."

Buzz dropped the subject. "You live around here?"

"Passing through," Natty answered shortly.

"By yourself?"

"Me and him."

"Just the two of you, huh?"

Natty nodded. She looked over her shoulder. The wolf was staring in at them.

Buzz reached a crossroad and turned off the highway.

"This the right way?" asked Natty.

"Shortcut," replied Buzz. "Saves hours on this road."

He drove on. "You're a pretty little thing, you know." He casually dropped his right hand from the steering wheel and stretched it across the back of the seat.

Natty jerked away from it. The wolf pressed his face against the glass. Natty glanced at him and saw that he was snarling again.

"You sure this is the right way?" she asked uneasily.

Buzz nodded. Then he put his arm around Natty.

"Hey!" she exclaimed.

"Come on now," said Buzz. "I'm just being friendly." He inched his hand down her arm.

The wolf pawed furiously at the window.

Natty wrenched away, and suddenly the wolf hurled his body at the window, shattering the glass. He leaped into the cab of the truck. Buzz tried to drive the truck and wrestle with the wolf. The truck swerved from side to side, tires screeching.

The wolf had just gotten a good grip on Buzz's arm when Natty managed to open her door. She barely noticed the speed with which the truck was roaring down the road. She just gathered her courage and jumped.

The wolf followed and raced to Natty, checking to be sure she was all right. Natty hugged the wolf quickly as Buzz's truck weaved down the road. Then she and the wolf ran back to the main highway to continue their lonely journey.

In Washington, Sol had returned to his job at the mill, bitter and sad.

"Any luck?" his boss asked him when he appeared in the mill office.

"Yeah," said Sol angrily. "Sure. I found her. She's right here. Can't you see?"

His boss shrugged, embarrassed. "I was just asking."

"Can I get back to work now?" asked Sol.

"Yeah. Yeah, sure." The boss stared after Sol as he strode out of the office.

Natty and the wolf found train tracks heading west and decided to follow them. Early one morning, as they crossed a rickety trestle, the wolf began sniffing the air, and Natty saw wisps of smoke rising from below. They walked on suspiciously.

Presently, Natty saw that they had come to a hobo camp. It was one of the biggest she'd ever seen. Sixty or seventy men were clustered in groups around small shelters of cardboard and scrap wood.

A shiver ran down Natty's spine. She was starving and knew she would find food here, but she remembered the hobos she had met on the train leaving Chicago and knew she would have to be careful.

She tiptoed down the wooden steps that led to the trestle and stood uncertainly at the edge of the camp. One hobo, not far from her, seemed to be apart from the others. He was cooking a pot of beans over a small fire. Natty breathed in deeply. She hadn't eaten since the day before, and those beans smelled wonderful. When the hobo left to gather more wood for his fire, Natty made her move. She rushed forward and grabbed the pot by its handle.

But as she turned to run, someone grabbed her.

"Let me go!" Natty shrieked, kicking and struggling.

The hobo held her tightly. "They're mine," he said.

Natty squirmed around and got a good look at the hobo's face. She stopped struggling. "I know you," she said in surprise. It was Harry Slade.

He let go of her and held his hand out, waiting for Natty to return the beans. "Hand them over," he said darkly.

Natty handed them over.

Harry let go of her, turned his back, and sat down by the fire.

"You helped me," Natty went on. "In Chicago. Remember?"

"Nice way of paying me back," replied Harry.

"I didn't know it was you."

"Doesn't make it right," he said, glancing at her over his shoulder.

Natty shrugged. She scanned the camp, looking for another chance to take some food.

"I wouldn't try it," Harry said, watching her. "Steal their food and they'll eat you up."

Natty shrugged again. Then she looked at the beans, which were now bubbling over.

"Got a spoon?" Harry asked her.

Natty shook her head.

Looking disgusted, Harry tossed his own spoon to her. "Go on."

"What do I have to do for it?" Natty asked warily.

"Just eat the beans, kid."

Natty didn't waste another second. She gulped them down. While she ate, the wolf appeared at the edge of the clearing, watching Natty's every move.

"Friend of yours?" asked Harry.

Natty turned and saw the wolf. "Where were you?" she asked him accusingly. "I could've been killed." The wolf whined. Then he trotted over to her and lay down. He wasn't growling, Natty noticed, so Harry must be okay.

"We're going to Washington," she told Harry.

"It's hard enough without packing a dog."

"He's a wolf."

"Oh, that's even better."

"We can take care of ourselves." Natty offered the wolf a spoonful of beans, and he lapped them up gratefully.

"Yeah, I see that," said Harry. "But, hey,

you're not my worry. I go alone. No partners. 'Specially not a girl."

"Well, nobody asked you," Natty retorted.

"Good. Don't."

"I won't."

At that moment, the wolf jumped to his feet. He stared through the camp, growling, his fur standing on end.

"Did you hear that?" Natty cried. "Something's not right."

"What?" said Harry.

"Something's wrong. He always knows."

Harry listened. Then he tensed, like the wolf, and began gathering up his belongings. "Beat it, kid," he said.

"Why?"

Harry didn't answer. He streaked to the edge of the camp and ducked behind a dilapidated building, half-hidden under the train trestle. Natty and the wolf went after him. They peered out into the hobo camp.

Behind them, a large group of men wearing crisp blue uniforms thundered into the camp on horseback. Some of them swung baseball bats at the hobos. Others threw torches and began to burn down the camp.

Natty and Harry watched. Natty was horrified, but Harry had seen it all before.

"Who are they?" Natty gasped.

"Main Streeters. Good, law-abiding citizens," Harry said.

"But why are they doing this?" asked Natty. "We weren't hurting anyone."

"They're scared of what we've got," said Harry. "Poverty. They think it's catching." He stood and started to walk away. Then he turned around. "You coming?" he asked Natty.

"But I thought . . ."

"Make up your mind, kid."

Harry started off again. Natty and the wolf ran after him.

At dawn the following morning, Natty, Harry, and the wolf were waiting by the railroad tracks Natty had followed the day before. From far down the tracks, a whistle blew. And from the woods came a howl. The wolf pricked his ears.

Soon the train pulled into view.

"Okay, kid," said Harry. "That's a through freight. Right train. Right speed. Get set."

Natty nodded. She was ready.

But the wolf stared into the woods, whining. When he heard another howl, he took off.

"Come back!" Natty shouted desperately. The wolf stopped for a second. Then he disappeared into the trees.

The train was passing them slowly. Harry

made a dash for the boxcars. "Come on!" he yelled to Natty. "The train won't wait." He leaped into a car, then reached his hand down to her.

Natty looked at Harry, then back to the woods as she ran alongside the train. "I can't leave the wolf!" she cried.

"Forget it," said Harry. "That was a she-wolf calling him. He's gone."

"No," answered Natty. "He wouldn't do that."

"Come on!" yelled Harry. The train was picking up speed. "Give me your hand!"

Natty looked to the woods once more, but she couldn't see any sign of the wolf. How could he do this to her? Would he really just leave her like this?

The wolf was gone, and Harry would quickly disappear down the tracks if Natty didn't do something. Natty didn't want to be left alone. She reached up, and Harry swung her into the boxcar. Then they both continued to watch the woods, and as they did the wolf burst from among the trees and raced after the train.

"I see him!" cried Natty. "He's coming, he's coming."

Harry shook his head. "He won't make it."

The train had picked up speed, and the wolf was a good distance away. But he pounded along, keeping pace with the train, his powerful muscles driving him forward. He drew even with Natty and Harry, gauged the speed of the train, then made a spectacular leap through the air and landed in their boxcar with a crash.

"He made it!" exclaimed Harry. "He made it!"

Chapter Ten

The train traveled steadily westward. Late one night, it slowed its pace and pulled into the station at a tiny town. In their boxcar, Harry and Natty slept soundly.

But suddenly Harry awoke with a start.

Voices drifted in from outside.

Natty awoke, too. "What is it?" she asked Harry.

"Shh!" he said urgently. He crept to the edge of the car and peeped out.

Two railroad detectives, "deeks," stopped at the next car and banged on it with their billy clubs. "Come out of there," one commanded.

A frightened hobo emerged from the car, and one of the deeks grabbed him and led him away roughly.

Natty stood up to see what Harry was looking at—and tripped over a metal pipe.

CLANK!

Harry seized her and pulled her into the shadows, signaling her to keep quiet. But one of the deeks had heard her.

"What was that?" he asked.

"What?"

"I heard something." The deek shone his flashlight around the boxcar where Harry and Natty huddled together, barely breathing. Natty could feel Harry's heart pounding in his chest. She glanced at him. She'd never been this close to a boy before.

The wolf growled softly. He stepped around a stack of cartons and peered out of the train.

"There," said the deek.

"It's just a dog," the other replied scornfully. "Let's go."

The deeks disappeared down the tracks.

But Harry and Natty remained where they were, wrapped in each other's arms. Harry's eyes searched Natty's. Then, suddenly self-conscious, they let go of each other. Harry crossed to the door of the boxcar.

"Are they gone?" Natty whispered.

"What?" said Harry. "Oh. Yeah."

Natty moved close to Harry again, but he

sidestepped her. "Come on, kid. Quit slowing me down."

Natty turned away, confused.

Sol Gann was hard at work. Strapped not far off the ground to the trunk of a tree, he and another lumberjack sawed and chopped. They were felling huge pines in a remote area of forest high up on a mountain in Washington. Nearby, Riley, a "topper," was perched a hundred and twenty feet up a massive pine, sawing the limbs off the tree before the other lumberjacks would chop it down. A rope was looped around his waist and tied to the tree. On his boots were spurs, which he dug into the bark of the tree as he worked his way up.

As Riley hacked through the last of the tree's limbs, he yelled, *"Tim-ber!"*

Sol and the others looked up. "Coming down! Watch yourself!" they shouted as the limb crashed to the forest floor.

Above them, Riley began to saw off the top of the tree, but as it fell over it cracked below him, and Riley went with it, a scream of terror escaping from his lips as he plummeted to the ground.

Sol and several of the lumberjacks saw him and raced to where he lay pinned under the treetop.

The boss ran over to them. "You'll be okay,

Riley," he said as the men carefully pulled him from under the trunk and loaded him onto a stretcher. But he wasn't at all sure that Riley would be okay.

The boss turned to the men who were watching solemnly. "All right, all right. Nothing we can do for him standing around. Let's go. Back to work."

He walked across the work site.

Sol went after him. "Too bad," he said.

"Yep."

"I guess you'll be needing a new topper."

"Uh huh."

"Well?" asked Sol.

"Well what?"

"Let me do it."

"It's widow's work," said the boss. "The most dangerous job up here."

"I'm not married."

"What are you trying to prove, Gann?" The boss knew all about Natty, but he didn't want Sol doing anything foolish.

"Just give me the job," said Sol.

The boss considered. "All right," he said at last. "It's yours."

Sol nodded and went back to work.

"Hey!" the boss yelled after him. "It won't bring your daughter back."

Sol pretended not to hear. He walked on.

* * *

Natty and Harry and the wolf stuck together. They stayed on the train till it reached the end of its run. Then they hopped off and began walking again. This time they walked along a deserted dirt road through a heavily wooded area.

The weather had turned even colder, and the gray, misty day brought out the reds and yellows of the leaves, making the trees around them more brilliant than ever.

But Natty didn't notice the scenery. "I'm hungry," she complained.

Harry shook his head. "You've got no business on the road, kid."

"I've got as much as you've got," Natty snapped.

"All right, all right."

They continued to walk, climbing higher. After several hours, the air seemed to grow colder and more damp with each step they took.

"You know," commented Natty, "it's beginning to snow."

"Really," said Harry sarcastically.

"Really."

The snow fell more thickly and covered the leaf-laden trees. It turned the ground to mud and clung to Harry and Natty's hair.

"I'm cold," said Natty.

"Buck up, kid."

"I'm bucking, I'm bucking."

Then Harry chucked a snowball at her, and Natty threw one back. Laughing and gasping for breath, they walked on. The light snow stopped, and the air grew warmer again. On one side of their road towered misty, snow-capped mountains. On the other side was a sparkling lake, reflecting the slate gray of the sky.

"Look at this," said Harry. "We got everything. Clean air, mountains, lakes."

"Lakes," scoffed Natty. "We got a lake five times this size in Chicago."

"Chicago, huh? I passed through once. It was night. Couldn't see much."

"You ain't seen Chicago, you ain't seen nothing," said Natty.

"You're a real woman of the world, kid," replied Harry, and he and Natty laughed again.

Late that day, Natty, Harry, and the wolf came to a large barn. Harry looked inside. "Come on," he said. "It's empty. Nobody here but a pig."

They plopped themselves down on a pile of hay and closed their eyes gratefully. The wolf dozed protectively by Natty.

"Harry?" Natty asked lazily.

"Hmm?"

"You awake?"

"No, kid. I'm talking in my sleep."

"I'm not really a kid, you know."

Harry didn't answer.

"I'm almost as old as you."

Harry rolled over on his side.

"Harry?" Natty asked him again.

"What?"

"Don't you ever feel like talking?"

"No!"

"Harry?"

"WHAT?"

"What'll you do when we get there? To Seattle?"

Harry gave up trying to sleep. He sat up. "Look for work," he told Natty.

"Have you been to the Coast before?"

Harry nodded slowly. "Four years ago. San Francisco." He drew in his breath slowly; his voice grew hushed. "Me and my old man. We were outside this refinery. Hundreds of us guys. A foreman came out. He said, 'I need two guys for the bull gang. Two guys for the hole.' He had four jobs," Harry went on. "Four lousy jobs. Everybody started pushing and shoving. My old man got knocked down. I couldn't get to him. There were so many guys. He never got up."

Natty reached her hand out to Harry. "I'm sorry," she said.

"Me too."

The wolf jumped to attention, and Harry grabbed Natty's hand and pulled her to her feet. Not even daring to see what the wolf had heard, they dashed out of the barn and ran across a field until they came to a water tank. Train tracks ran below the tank. Harry looked at them, looked at the tank, and got an idea. He began explaining it to Natty.

Soon they were climbing the rough wooden staircase that led to the top of the tower. The wolf followed behind. When they reached the top, Natty peered anxiously over the edge. It was a long way down.

"Don't look down," said Harry.

"Right," replied Natty, but she couldn't look away.

A train was approaching.

"When she slows up," Harry told Natty, "you walk down the arm, then let yourself go."

"Right," said Natty again, even more uncertainly. She looked along the narrow wooden arm hinged to the outside of the tower. When pulled down, it would hang out over the track below. Harry wanted her to walk along *that?*

"You can do it," said Harry.

"Absolutely."

The train drew closer.

"Okay. Get set." Harry tensed, then scrambled to the roof of the tower, dropped onto the arm below, and swung it down as the train roared along underneath him.

Natty began to inch her way along the arm, but her legs seemed frozen. She could barely move.

"Come on!" shouted Harry. "One step at a time."

"Right." Natty inched a bit further, clutching for supports.

"Don't look down . . . and don't pull that wire!" Harry continued shouting at her. "No, no, no! Let go of that wire!"

It was too late. Natty had grabbed at a cable attached to the arm and let loose a torrent of water from inside the tower. It poured out, washing Harry and Natty down into an open train car filled with sawdust.

They looked at each other and burst out laughing. Then they looked up to find the wolf watching them from the top of the water tower. They called to him frantically.

He hesitated, then jumped, soaring through

the air, and landed in the next car. He made another leap into their car, and as the train sped westward Natty and Harry whooped victoriously and petted and praised the wolf, who sat between them panting happily.

Chapter Eleven

It was a clear, sunny day when Harry, Natty, and the wolf arrived in Seattle. They headed straight for the huge government buildings downtown.

"Where do I start?" Natty asked Harry. She felt penned in by the imposing buildings that surrounded them. They seemed to rise out of the sidewalk, and Natty thought they looked alien and somehow wrong after her weeks in the mountains and woods.

"Let's find the WPA office," suggested Harry.

Natty nodded. That made sense. Sol's job was probably WPA. The government had created the Works Progress Administration especially to help the unemployed during the Depression.

After asking several people where the office

was, Natty and Harry were given directions to a building not far away. The wolf trotted along at Natty's side, and Natty could feel the tension in his muscles. She knew he was uncomfortable on the crowded city streets.

They reached the building, and Harry decided to wait outside. A table had been set up at the base of the wide stone steps. Behind the table, a man and a woman were signing people up for WPA work. Harry watched them curiously as Natty and the wolf climbed the steps.

A half an hour later, Natty came running back down the steps, a huge grin on her face. As she ran toward Harry, he realized that Natty had changed, even in the short time he had known her. Her hair was longer, and she looked less tomboyish . . . prettier.

"Harry! Harry! Look at this," Natty cried. She shoved a piece of paper at him. "It's a WPA project. A lumber camp. I got us a ride to the mill."

"The mill?" Harry glanced at the paper.

"Don't you get it? My dad's probably up there."

"So what? What if he is?"

"I don't understand what you—"

"He ran out on you, Natty," Harry said, cutting her off.

"No! No, he didn't. You're wrong."

"Am I? Look, Natty, I got work—in California." He pointed to the man and the woman assigning WPA jobs.

"That's . . . great," Natty said slowly. She knew Harry had wanted a job on the West Coast.

"I want you to come with me," said Harry. "We'll go in style. We'll take the bus! What do you say?"

For a moment, Natty looked excited. Harry really wanted her to come with him. He liked her. But she remembered Sol, and her face fell.

"Hey, it's no sweat off my back either way," said Harry quickly. "I just thought—"

"I've got to find him first," Natty interrupted. "Before I can do anything. I just can't go with you now, understand? Please understand."

Harry looked down. He nodded. He knew he had lost Natty. But he did understand.

Harry and Natty stood inside the bus depot in Seattle. They paced back and forth nervously, not speaking, but glancing at each other every now and then. Harry's bus pulled up. The driver swung the door open.

"Guess you better get on," said Natty. "Don't want them to leave without you." She smiled sadly at Harry.

"Right."

"I guess it's really goodbye, huh?" she said, her voice quavering.

"I guess so."

"Take care of yourself."

"You too," replied Harry.

"Okay."

Harry turned and started to climb onto the bus.

"Harry!" Natty called suddenly.

He turned around hopefully, daring to believe that Natty had changed her mind.

She hadn't, but she moved close to him and lifted her face, her lips brushing his. They kissed tenderly.

Then Harry pulled away, smiled, and climbed onto the bus. He sat next to a window. As the bus drove off, he and Natty stared at each other. They didn't drop their eyes until the bus turned a corner.

When the bus was out of sight, the wolf glanced at Natty, then stuck his nose in her hand and whined mournfully. He would miss Harry, too.

Chapter Twelve

Natty and the wolf threaded their way through the bus depot to the gate, where they would wait for their ride to the mill. Natty was glad to think she was so close to finding Sol, because it took some of the hurt out of leaving Harry.

When she reached the mill, Natty went directly to the main office. A tough-looking woman wearing men's clothes was in charge of the office. Her name was Mack. Natty watched her as she ordered workers here and there, shouting her instructions above the noise.

Finally she noticed Natty. "Yeah? What do you want?" she barked.

"I'm looking for someone. My dad," replied Natty.

"He's at the mill?"

"I think so. Sol Gann."

Mack began flipping through cards in a file cabinet. "G-A-N-N?" she spelled out.

Natty nodded.

Mack looked through the cards a second time, then slammed the drawer shut. "There's no Gann."

"He's got to be here," Natty said, scared. She opened her locket and showed it to Mack. "There. That's him," she said urgently. "See? Do you know him?"

Mack studied the picture but shook her head. "Look, they move a lot of guys through here. It's almost impossible to keep track. Half the time we don't know who's here, who's at Base Camp, who's anywhere."

"What's Base Camp?"

"Forget it, kid. You can't go up there."

"But . . ."

"Sorry. There's nothing I can do for ya." Mack started to turn around, then noticed the wolf for the first time. "Hey, what's he doing in here? Get him out of here."

Natty hurried out of the office.

Far up the mountain at Base Camp, a group of lumberjacks sat in a tent, waiting excitedly. They had worked long and hard. Now they were about to be paid and given a short holiday before it was time to return to work. Sol sat with the men, the only one who seemed not to care about the vacation.

The boss entered the tent, and the men followed him with their eyes.

"So what's the word, boss? When do we get outta here?" asked one.

"I thought we were finished on this mountain," said another.

The boss shook his head. "They're sending us back up."

The men stared. They began shouting.

"They can't do that! We just came down."

"One more job," replied the boss. "Then we're out of here for good. But it's tricky. We're using nitro."

The room became quiet. Nitro. Nitroglycerin. A powerful explosive. One accident, and the men could all be killed. And they knew it. They also knew they would be paid well.

"Double wages for the lead men," said the boss. "Any volunteers?"

Sol was the first to raise his hand.

Natty and the wolf hid in the shadows of a building by the mill office and watched Mack close up her office and walk away. As she headed toward the main gate, she passed a supply truck.

"Hey, Mack," called a worker. "How come I

always have to drive these things up the mountain?"

"You lookin' to get fired?" Mack shouted back. "'Cause I'll be up there to check on you."

The worker backed down. "Base Camp by breakfast, Mack," he assured her.

Natty smiled when she heard this. She and the wolf waited until Mack and the worker were gone. Then they streaked toward the supply truck, climbed quietly into the back, and hid under a tarpaulin.

Natty and the wolf reached Base Camp early the next morning—five minutes after Sol's team left for the mountaintop with their supply of nitro. When the truck that Natty was riding in came to a stop, she peeped out from under the tarp. Then she waited until the coast was clear, jumped down, and, with the wolf at her side, began running through the camp, searching the faces for Sol's. She walked along until she almost ran into someone.

Mack.

"What are you doing?" Mack demanded angrily. "I told you not to come up here. This country's for him." She nodded at the wolf. "Not for a girl. You're going back down. First truck I line up."

Natty swallowed hard. She was sure she was

near Sol now. They had to let her find him. They just had to. But Mack led Natty to a table in the mess tent and told her to stay there.

Natty sat and stared at the wolf, wondering why he was so restless. He would pace back and forth, lie at Natty's feet, get up, and pace again. Once, he ran to the tent flap and stood at attention, his ears pricked forward. Then he relaxed and returned to Natty, lying down with a sigh.

Natty pulled a postcard from her pocket and began writing a note to Harry.

"Dear Harry. I'm okay, I guess. So's the wolf. How's California? I haven't found my dad yet. I miss you."

Natty paused, sucking on the end of her pencil. How should she sign the card? *Love? . . .* No. *Yours truly? . . . Sincerely?*

"*Natty,*" she said aloud finally. "Just plain *Natty.*"

As Natty wrote her name, she heard a loud, mournful howl from the woods beyond the mess tent. The wolf was on his feet in an instant, ears forward, eyes practically boring a hole through the tent.

Natty watched him fearfully.

The wolf whined. He looked at Natty, whined again, then turned his attention back to the woods. His whole body was quivering.

The silence was pierced by another long howl. It was a she-wolf.

And suddenly the wolf could stand it no longer. He raced through the tent flap. Horrified, Natty went after him. But the wolf was much too fast for her. He tore across the camp toward the woods. Natty watched him, her heart pounding in her chest. Then she put her thumb and finger in her mouth and whistled shrilly.

The wolf slowed. He stopped and turned to Natty. Natty ran to him and hugged him hard, smiling with relief. She started back to the mess tent, but the wolf wasn't following her. He was looking at the woods and whining.

Natty felt cold fear washing over her.

Another howl came from the woods, and once more the wolf began to quiver.

Natty knew what she had to do. She knelt by the wolf and stroked his head. "Go on," she told him. "You belong out there. It's time."

The wolf looked at her and whined.

"I'll be all right," said Natty. Her eyes were filled with tears, but she wouldn't let them fall. "Go on. *Go!*"

The wolf hesitated for just a second, staring into Natty's eyes. Then he turned and ran.

Chapter Thirteen

Natty stood outside the mess tent, feeling very small and alone. She had lost Sol, she had lost Harry, and now—unbelievably—she had lost the wolf. She allowed herself to cry briefly. Then she returned to the tent to wait for Mack.

She stood quickly when she heard a voice call, "Hey, you still in there?"

Before Natty could answer, Mack burst inside, a grin on her face, saying excitedly, "I think I might have found him!"

"What?" Natty was almost afraid to believe it.

"Now, don't get your hopes up," Mack went on, holding out an envelope, "but is this you?"

Natty took the envelope. It was addressed to Miss Natty Gann at the San Marco Hotel, and stamped across the front in red ink were the words RETURN TO SENDER.

Natty began breathing more quickly. She ripped the envelope open and read the letter inside.

"Dear Natty," it said. "Leaving was the hardest thing I've ever done. It tears at my guts to think I've let you down. I hope you can forgive me. I love you. Come right away. Dad."

Natty could feel something else in the envelope. She reached inside and pulled out a train ticket—one-way from Chicago to Seattle. Sol hadn't left her! Not really. He'd sent for her, just as he'd promised!

"Where is he?" Natty cried.

"With D-Group," said Mack. "They took off this morning. They should still be up the mountain. I got you a ride there."

The men in D-Group had reached the mountaintop safely and were almost finished with their dangerous job. Sol was packing a load of nitro into a bag marked with a skull and crossbones. He worked swiftly and confidently.

But Rocky, one of the other lead men, was having trouble. He loaded his bag nervously, his hands shaking, sweat forming on his upper lip.

Sol looked up and watched him. "You don't have to do this, Rocky. I can cover for you."

"Thanks, Sol," said Rocky gratefully, "but I'll be all right."

Sol nodded encouragingly at him. "Sure you will. Just one step at a time, huh?"

Rocky managed a smile, but it faded quickly. He picked up his bag gingerly and followed Sol. They joined the other lead men as they fanned out across the area, setting their charges at the bases of thick trees.

A little distance away, the boss and the rest of the crew watched anxiously.

Natty's ride left immediately, and she could barely contain herself as the truck rolled slowly up the mountain, traveling back and forth on the switchbacks, negotiating one hairpin turn after another.

Natty rode in the back of the truck, in the open air. "Come on, come on," she urged the driver under her breath. "Faster."

And at that second a tire blew out, the brakes screeched, and the truck drew to a bumpy stop at the side of the road. The driver jumped out, and Natty scrambled down to examine the tire with him.

"Can you fix it?" she asked.

The driver pulled his cap off, scratched his head, and shrugged.

Natty could have belted him one. Why wouldn't he hurry up?

He pulled a jack out of the truck and began to change the tire. He seemed to be working in slow motion. Finally, Natty couldn't stand it any longer. She raced up the road as fast as her legs could carry her, calling a breathless "Thanks anyway, Mister" over her shoulder as she ran.

Further up the mountain, Sol's boss and the crew waited for the sound of the first explosion. When it came, it echoed through the hills like thunder, shaking the ground. Another explosion followed, and another. Dirt and debris rained down on the crew, and the air filled with smoke.

The boss looked at his men. His eyes were wide with disbelief. "That was too big," he told them shakily. "Way too big."

He jumped into action. "Get those guys outta there!" he shouted to his crew, struggling to be heard over the noise.

Natty, still running up the road, stumbled with surprise at the rumble of the first explosion. Then she picked up her pace, running faster than ever.

At the explosion site, the crew scrambled madly to gather the injured lead men and load them carefully into the truck. They ran from one worker to the other, trying to see who was most badly injured, who needed medical attention the fastest. They dragged bloody bodies across the ground or draped moaning men between their shoulders.

When at last the wounded men were loaded in the truck, the boss yelled to the driver, "Get them down! Fast! Go!"

The tires squealed as the truck pulled away.

Not far down the road, Natty was still pounding along. She reached one of the hairpin turns, and just as she was about to round it, a truck came barreling toward her. Natty jumped for the side of the road and turned to watch the truck as it roared past. She gasped. She could see in the open back. The truck was filled with injured men.

Natty stared, horrified. One of the men was slumped over, his cap pulled low over his eyes. But Natty recognized him immediately. She raced down the road after the truck.

"Dad! Dad!" she cried.

But the driver of the truck couldn't hear Natty, and he sped on his way, the distance between Sol and Natty quickly growing wider.

Immediately, Natty cut straight down through the woods beside the road. It was faster than going back and forth. Maybe she could catch the truck as it came around the next turn.

Inside the truck, Sol looked up. Funny, he thought he had heard something. He searched the road behind him.

Gasping and panting, Natty reached the leg of the road below her, hoping she had beaten the truck. She looked from side to side—and there was the truck disappearing in the distance. It was still ahead of her.

Natty watched it, tears filling her eyes. *"No! No!"* she screamed. She turned and looked up the road in the other direction.

Then she blinked her eyes and looked again. Was it really—

Sol!

It *was* Sol. His arm was cut and bleeding, and his shirt was torn, but it was her father. He was really there.

He and Natty raced toward each other, arms outstretched. When they met, Sol caught Natty in a joyful embrace and swung her around and around. Natty cried, and Sol cried. They kissed, and then they began to laugh.

And they never knew that above them, perched on a rock, the wolf looked on, panting contentedly, watching them with his wise yellow eyes.

About the Author

ANN MATTHEWS grew up in Princeton, New Jersey, and was graduated from Smith College. She lives in New York City where she is a writer and free-lance editor of children's books.

Under the name Ann M. Martin, she has written BUMMER SUMMER, INSIDE OUT, JUST YOU AND ME, STAGE FRIGHT, and ME AND KATIE (THE PEST), a sequel to STAGE FRIGHT.

In her spare time, she enjoys reading and needlework. She loves cats, and has an orange tabby named Mouse.

Would you like to see more of

The Journey of

NATTY GANN

Read Little Simon's THE JOURNEY OF NATTY GANN STORYBOOK. This 64-page hardcover book is full of color photographs from the Walt Disney Pictures film. You can see for yourself how Natty finds the wolf . . . rides the freight trains . . . escapes from reform school . . . and survives her cross-country journey in search of her father. You will see Natty, Sol, Harry and the wolf, and enjoy the action and adventure of THE JOURNEY OF NATTY GANN.

__THE JOURNEY OF NATTY GANN 60502/$7.95

Look for the storybook at your bookstore, or send in the coupon below.

224